DRIFTING FROM DEADWOOD

PIONEER BRIDES OF RATTLESNAKE RIDGE
BOOK SIX

RAMONA FLIGHTNER

GRIZZLY DAMSEL PUBLISHING

Kristen, your constant encouragement
and faith in me motivated me as I wrote this novel.
Thank you for your wonderful friendship.

ABOUT DRIFTING FROM DEADWOOD:

Will these two opposites find a way to make a home—and a life—together?

Eleanor Ferguson has little faith in the promises of men after her husband's death leaves her with a floundering ranch and two growing boys. Her top priority is to create a legacy for her sons, but a greedy neighbor has other plans. When a drifter answers her help wanted ad, she doesn't expect to feel attraction for the handsome stranger.

Lance Gallagher drifts from ranch to ranch until life leads him to Rattlesnake Ridge, Nevada. He's willing to work for low wages on the Ferguson ranch until the mines deliver on their promise of a payout. The more time Lance spends with Eleanor and her sons, however, the more attracted he finds himself to the lovely widow. Unwilling to risk his heart, he makes plans to leave.

Then tragedy strikes, forcing Eleanor and Lance to rely on each other. Can they overcome their fears and learn to trust in love again?

PROLOGUE

W anted: *A competent ranch hand willing to work long hours for room and board. Preferred young, energetic single male. Enquire at the Broken Pine Ranch. Speak with E. Ferguson.*

CHAPTER 1

June 1877, Rattlesnake Ridge, Nevada

Eleanor Ferguson held up a hand to shield her eyes from the glaring sunlight as she watched the approach of Sterling Hayden. He cantered his horse down her long drive, and she pasted on a deferential smile as she waited to greet him. His once-monthly visits had evolved into weekly visits, and she feared they would soon turn into daily visits. She said a silent prayer that today's visit would be a short one.

As she awaited his arrival, she took deep, calming breaths and focused on her ranch, the Broken Pine. The corrals near the barn were in need of shoring up, and the barn's roof would be lucky to make it through another winter. However, she saw past all the work to the long, golden grass blowing in the breeze, the rolling hills leading to the mountains in the distance that remained snowcapped in mid-June. The distant fields with her cattle scattered over them. She nodded her head in satisfaction as she focused again on the man nearing her ranch house.

Eleanor swiped a hand down her serviceable brown calico dress and patted at her brown hair with red highlights, ensuring it was tied back in a tidy knot. Clasping her hands at her waist, she fought the urge to fidget as the large man dismounted his black and white pinto horse. He tied the reins to the hitching post, swaggered toward Eleanor, and tipped his hat in her direction. A large man, his presence would have overwhelmed her had she not been standing on the top step of her porch. "Mr. Hayden," she murmured. "How thoughtful of you to visit us today."

His chest puffed out, and he clasped his hands at his Sunday-best burgundy waistcoat. "I've always considered myself thoughtful. And generous." He waited for her agreement, frowning when her smile appeared as an attempt to conceal a grimace. He reached into his waistcoat, extracting a slip of paper. "I was disturbed to read this in the *Rattlesnake Ridge*

Recorder. I spoke with Samuel Langhorne, but he insisted you had published it." He shook the paper at her as he spoke.

"I assume you are referring to my desire for a competent ranch hand?" Eleanor asked with a raised eyebrow. "As you can see, my need for more help is evident." She held her palms up as though in supplication of aid and then crossed them over her waist again. "It should come as no surprise to you that I am in need of workers."

"Workers?" he sputtered at the plural form of the word, scratching at his thick brown hair with gray at the temples, pushing his hat nearly off. "I've told you, dear Mrs. Ferguson. If you are in need of aid, I am only too happy to help you."

She flushed and looked down as though in a demure manner. "And I thank you for your solicitousness. However, as you know, running a ranch is a full-time endeavor, and I need my own men." She smiled in an attempt to soften the forcefulness of her words. "It gives me tremendous comfort to know I have such an excellent neighbor who I can call on, should the need arise."

Sterling's chest puffed out again at her praise, and he focused on the buildings near the ranch house. The peeling paint on the barn. The patch-work-shingled barn roof. The chicken coop fence on the verge of collapse. "If you don't mind me saying, Mrs. Ferguson, you need a man around here who knows about the running of a ranch. It's too much for a woman to attempt to tackle."

She nodded again. "I shall consider your counsel."

He beamed at her before tugging her hand to his, raising it and kissing it. "I look forward to our next visit." He slammed his hat back in place before sauntering to his dozing horse.

As she watched him ride away, her shoulders relaxed, and she let out a deep breath. "How much of it did you hear, Zachariah?" she asked.

A deep chuckle sounded from inside the house. "All of it. Puffed-up buffoon." Zachariah O'Neill stepped outside, allowing the screen door to slam shut behind him. He stood at nearly six feet tall and half a foot taller than Eleanor, with broad shoulders and a penetrating gaze. Few called him friend, but those who did knew him to be loyal and trustworthy.

"I fear he'll persist until he gets what he wants," she whispered, shuddering.

"You aren't marrying him," Zachariah snapped. "I'll marry you before that happens." He fought a grimace, and then they grinned at each other before they burst out laughing.

"Oh, Zachariah, you are good medicine." She laughed as she looped her hand through his arm. "I can't imagine us married. We're too much like brother and sister."

He winked at her. "Let's hope we find a way to foil that man. He's too intent on you." His gaze sharpened on the retreating form of Sterling Hayden. "I could always shoot him."

She rolled her eyes. "You aren't shooting anyone, especially not him." She shuddered again. "I couldn't run this ranch without you. And I couldn't handle any more scandal." Her eyes shadowed for a moment before she focused on her friend and foreman.

"Well, I'll tell you what needs to be shot." He lost any levity as he glared toward the hills and mountains. "Another calf was found dead this morning."

"What?" Eleanor gasped as she gripped his arm. "We can't continue to lose cattle, Zachariah."

He jerked his head in agreement. "Seems the wolves we killed last month weren't the correct pack. Or another pack moved into their territory."

She rubbed at her forehead. "That makes eight so far this summer," she said. "If cattle prices remain low like last year …" She shook her head with frustration as she looked out at her ranchland.

Zachariah squeezed her arm and smiled at her. "You're smart and resourceful, Eleanor. You won't lose this ranch." His smile turned cunning as he looked at her. "If the townsfolk only knew that you were the brains behind the ranch …" He chuckled.

"They have a hard-enough time understanding how a widow has been able to hold on for two years after her husband was shot dead playing a hand of cards at the saloon." She took a deep breath and closed her eyes, fighting a wave of bitterness as she thought about her husband, Alan, who had valued gambling more than his family or the ranch.

Zachariah shrugged. "Few understood you ran the ranch from the moment Alan obtained it. That you had the foresight to secure the water rights to your land. That you insisted on maintaining the timber rights."

She smiled at her friend, and some of her tension eased with his words. "We'll find a way, even if I have to cut some of our trees to sell to Mr. Winthrop. I had hoped to save that resource for my boys, but it's more important to have a ranch to give them. Besides, I'd rather deal with Mr. Winthrop than with Mr. Hayden." Jacob Winthrop was the founder of the nearby town, Rattlesnake Ridge, and the local timber baron. A successful businessman, he was known to be fair to his business partners. He was also the mayor of the thriving town.

She looked down the drive as another rider approached. "That's not Mr. Hayden returning," she murmured.

Zachariah squinted and shook his head as he studied the unfamiliar rider and horse. "And it's not one of his employees. I wonder who it could be?"

Lance Gallagher surveyed the land around him and the approaching ranch buildings as he neared the couple standing on the porch. He noted the dilapidated state of the structures, although they appeared to have been built soundly. He nodded with approval as little couldn't be fixed with hard work, a hammer, and a bucketful of nails. He took a deep breath of the fresh air with a hint of the distant pine forest and slowed his horse from a trot to a walk. The brilliant blue sky overhead with a few puffy white clouds, the soft breeze ruffling his horse's mane, and the birds chirping as they swooped overhead filled him with momentary peace.

Lance dismounted his horse, patted him on his neck, while murmuring his approval of his hard work, and tied the reins to a post. After a moment, he approached the wary couple waiting him on the front porch. "Hello, Mr. and Mrs. Ferguson," he said as he doffed his hat, revealing thick blond hair. He frowned as the woman stiffened, and the man bit back a chuckle. After a moment, he cleared his throat and said, "I'm Lance Gallagher, and I've come to talk with you about the ranch hand position."

The tall, self-possessed, black-haired man moved away from the poker-faced woman with her guarded blue-eyed gaze. "I'm Zachariah O'Neill, the foreman of the Broken Pine Ranch. Mrs. Ferguson is the owner."

Lance nodded his head in a deferential manner. "I beg your pardon, ma'am. I'm new to these parts, and I was unaware that you owned the ranch."

Her gaze narrowed as she saw his discomfort. "Does that mean you'll find it difficult to work for a woman?"

He flashed a smile, revealing a dimple in his left cheek. "No, ma'am. It's as I said. I meant no disrespect. I imagine you're as capable as anyone in the running of your spread." He looked over the acres with the cattle in the distance. "I've met many women in my travels who've had to run the farm or ranch after their men died in the War."

He saw her eyes cloud, but she failed to respond to his subtle probing comment.

Zachariah crossed his arms over his strong chest. "Why do you think we should take you on?"

Lance shrugged and scratched at a patch of skin behind his ear. "Well, for starters, if you don't get that barn roof fixed in the next few months, you won't have a place to shelter your horses or milk cows during the winter. The paddocks need attention, and the chicken coop looks as though a strong wind would shatter it to the ground. I imagine you'd not relish searching through the grass for eggs each morning." He met Zachariah's challenging stare. "It's nothing that time, sweat, and nails won't fix."

"The last man who wanted the job was concerned about painting the barn and ranch house," Eleanor said in a quiet voice. She met Lance's amused stare.

"What good is paint when the building's about to fall to the ground like a pile of matchsticks?" Lance shook his head as he looked over the property. "No, painting should wait," he murmured. His breath caught as a young black-haired boy emerged into the nearby paddock leading a fidgety palomino. "Easy," Lance said as he moved to the paddock with sure, strong strides.

He ducked through the fencing and approached the horse, now snorting and tossing its head. Lance made gentle clicks and spoke soothing words in a low tone. He held his hand out and waited for the horse to calm before he touched the horse's muzzle. "Go, son," he ordered. He heard the youngster scamper from the paddock as Lance continued to murmur his praise of the horse. After a moment, the horse gave a snort and relaxed. Scratching behind its ear, Lance laughed as it bumped his head against his chest.

"Seems you know your way around horses, too," Zachariah said. He leaned against the paddock railing with his arms slung over the top. The young boy stood beside him, the woman's arm wrapped over the boy's shoulder as she stood on the other side of the boy.

"I spent some time in the cavalry. And on a horse ranch," he said.

The woman let out a breathy sigh. "I'm thankful you did. Simon knows better than to approach the horses, and he's never to go near Spirit."

Lance scratched the horse again. "Spirit. A fitting

name." He looked at the chastened boy standing beside the woman who he presumed was his mother. "A boy must learn how to work with horses from a young age."

Simon brightened at the words, only remaining on the other side of the paddock fencing by his mother's firm grip. "See, Mama?" he said with youthful enthusiasm. "I told you I knew what I was doing!"

Lance gave a final pat to the horse and left him to wander to his water trough. "No, the problem is you didn't know what you were doing, and you need to learn. Much longer in there with that horse and there's every chance you would have been trampled."

Simon paled. "Like Mr. Bailey, one of the town drunks," he whispered. "His horse smashed him up good."

Eleanor looked at Lance with barely veiled frustration. "And I suppose you believe you could teach him how to care for a horse? How to never be in danger around a horse?"

Lance climbed over the paddock railing and shook his head. "No, ma'am. I can't promise you to always keep the boy safe. But I can help so he has less chance of coming to harm." He watched as the man called Zachariah shared a long look with Mrs. Ferguson.

"Fine," she whispered. "Although you'll have two boys following you around. My son, Simon"—she patted the black-haired boy's shoulder—"and my eldest son, Peter."

"Although you better not spend all your time with Mr. Gallagher," Zachariah said as he ruffled Simon's hair. "I'll still want to spend time with you."

"No one could replace you, Uncle Zachariah," Simon proclaimed loyally. He gazed at the horse with a deep longing.

"Let him be, boy. Tomorrow will be time to begin," Lance said. When Zachariah motioned for Lance to follow him, he nodded to Mrs. Ferguson.

They walked past the barn to a nearby bunkhouse with sagging roof. Zachariah kicked on the door a few times for it to open.

"This might be my first project," Lance muttered as he looked around the clean, but dilapidated space.

Zachariah smiled. "As long as there's no storm tonight, it shouldn't fall down over your head while you sleep."

Lance glanced around at the four cots with rolled-up mattresses on them and poked his head into a small kitchen. "Am I the only one here?"

Zachariah nodded. "We have a few men in the higher pastures during the summer. We'd hoped to make it through summer without needing more help. But, as you can see, we need it, or the place will fall down around our ears. I can't do all the repairs that need to be done."

Lance scratched behind his ear again. "I had thought I'd work with horses or be with the herd."

"Work is work." Zachariah stood at his imposing height and waited for Lance to nod. "No need for you to cook for yourself. You'll join the family for dinner each night. The water pump is by the barn, and a creek's not too far away if you want a soak." He rubbed at his forehead. "Washday is Tuesday."

At the gentle knock, Lance looked to the door. "Mrs. Ferguson," he said deferentially and then reached for the overloaded basket she carried. "Thank you."

"That should help you settle in," she said as she took a deep breath after carrying the heavy basket from the house.

He looked at the hamper filled with blankets, sheets, and towels. "Thank you, ma'am." He watched as the foreman and Mrs. Ferguson left, talking softly as they walked toward the ranch house.

After Lance made his bed, he walked outside

and returned to his horse. He led Amaretto into the barn and into a stall. "I know, boy," he said when his horse snuffled as though in displeasure. "I'll clean it out properly for you tomorrow, and you'll live like a prince." Amaretto tossed his head as though he understood and snorted once before calming. Lance curried him, whistling the entire time.

When he finished, he wandered around the barn, finding a room with bins filled with oats, a tack room, and another room filled with odds and ends. Soon, he'd found a bag full of nails, lumber, and a hammer. He strapped on a tool belt and hefted a few pieces of lumber over one shoulder. When he arrived at the bunkhouse, he fought a smile at the presence of two boys poking through the basket on the floor.

"You mess up my bed, you make it," he said. He chuckled as they jumped at his voice. "I'm Lance," he said with a smile as they stared at him with wonder. "The new ranch hand."

"I'm Peter," the taller boy said as he angled himself in front of his brother. He had brown hair and hazel eyes.

"Nice to meet you, Peter. I already met your brother, Simon." He winked at the boy grinning at him from around his brother's shoulder. "Did you come to help me?"

Peter shrugged. "We ain't allowed to do much."

Lance frowned. "You're young men. You need to learn to work hard. And to speak properly." He looked at Peter pointedly, and the boy flushed. "Will you grab the bag of nails I left in the supply room in the barn? And then I'll need your help in here." He watched as the brothers raced to the barn and sighed as he imagined them fighting over the bag and scattering the nails over the barn floor. He shook his head and set the lumber on the floor.

While waiting for the boys to return, he studied the ceiling that dipped in the middle. The beam in the center of the roof appeared to sag, and he walked outside to see if anything was on the roof. He shook his head in confusion to find nothing there.

He turned when he heard the patter of little feet running toward him. "Mr. Lance! Mr. Lance!" Simon hollered. He held up the bag of nails, clutching the top closed so none flew out with his mad dash from the barn and his brother.

"What did you do to your brother?" Lance asked as he bit back a smile at the exuberant boy's antics.

Simon flushed and tried to look innocent. "I don't know what you mean."

"You're the young'un. Peter should have come back with the bag of nails." He fought another smile as pride, embarrassment, and satisfaction flit across Simon's face.

"I outsmarted him!" Simon said with a triumphant grin as he thrust the bag of nails at Lance.

Lance looked to the barn as Peter ran after his brother, his pursuit foiled when he saw Simon next to Lance. "I won't be around to protect you forever, lad," Lance whispered to Simon as he swallowed a laugh at the sight of Peter. The right side of Peter's body was covered in horse dung and hay.

"Boy, let's get you washed up. I might like horses, but I don't want my bunkhouse stinking of them," Lance called out to Peter. He led Peter to the water pump and helped him wash off the majority of the muck. "Go inside and change. I'll wait for you before I start my project." He watched as a sodden Peter dashed away.

"I was in a pile of cow manure last week," Simon said with a bright smile. "Isn't that what brothers do?"

Lance laughed and ruffled Simon's hair. "Now, Simon, why would my roof sag in the middle if there's nothing on it?"

"There's nothing on it *now*. But last winter we had us a bad storm. And half a tree landed on it." He pointed to the remnant of a pine tree a short distance away and reenacted the large limb crashing onto the roof. Simon's blue eyes gleamed with mischief. "The men inside screamed like babies and refused to go back inside. Said the home was *posseed*." He paused and shook his head. "Possessed." He nodded in triumph. "No men want to stay in that bunkhouse now."

Lance shook his head in confusion. "You have men working in the high country this summer."

"They'll only work in summer when they can sleep outside with cattle for company. Won't be here in winter. Won't do the work that needs to be done in the slow season. They think the ranch is cursed 'cause it's run by a woman ..."

"Simon, enough chattering," Peter said as he rejoined them.

Lance frowned at the abrupt interruption of Simon's story. "That was quick."

Peter puffed out his chest. "I know how to sneak in and out of the house without Mama seeing me. Otherwise, she'd still be scolding me."

"Well, come along," he said to his young helpers.

Soon, he was standing on a chair, with his arms

over his head as he pushed up against the sagging beam. Peter and Simon pushed one of the timbers in place as they followed his instructions. "Good work, lads," he said as he hopped down from the chair.

"It's crooked," Simon said as he tilted his head to the side to stare at the support timber that stood at an angle.

Lance smiled. "It is now, but it won't be for long. I need you to hold it steady at its base while I tap it into place up above." Soon the first support timber was in position, and the ceiling didn't sag quite as much.

Lance pointed to an area farther into the room. "Let's put one more up there. Then I'll know it won't come crashing down on me in the middle of the night."

Simon looked at him with surprise. "Aren't you afraid of it being possessed?"

"No," he said with a shrug. "I've seen enough in the real world to know my true enemy is man." He attempted a smile and then continued to shore up the roof with his two helpers.

When the boys left to clean up for supper, Lance wandered past the barn and walked a short way up the hill. The soft early evening breeze ruffled his hair, and he stared at the gently rolling hills that led to beautiful snowcapped peaks in the distance. He bowed his head as he attempted to relax and to allow the peace of the moment to fill him. After a few more minutes, he returned to the barn and washed up for dinner.

He arrived at the ranch house a half hour later after changing into his only clean shirt. When Simon answered the door, he relaxed. "Hello, Simon."

"You're here!" Simon called out. "He's here, Mama!" Simon ran away and then looked over his shoulder as though expecting Lance to follow him. When Lance entered the house and shut the door behind him, Simon raced toward a room at the back of the house. At the entrance, there was a staircase to the upstairs and two doorways off the hallway. He peered into the room to the right and saw a formal dining room with dark furniture that looked as though it hadn't been used in years. The larger living room to the right had a settee, a rocking chair, a comfortable wingback chair and a spinning wheel set by a fireplace. The wallpapered walls were covered in a subtle floral pattern with a cream-colored background. He followed Simon down the hallway into the back of the house with a large kitchen with room for a table. A back door led to the outside, and he saw a fenced kitchen garden through the windows.

"I'm sorry if I'm late," Lance murmured as he saw platters of food on the table.

"It's my fault," Eleanor said. "I never told you that dinner is at six." She glanced at the clock that chimed the half hour.

Zachariah entered and nodded at Lance. "I thought I'd have to find that old bell to call you in to dinner."

"I ... I wandered the ranch some and lost track of time." Lance ran a self-conscious hand over his clean shirt.

"Well, we're all together now. That's what matters," Eleanor said as she cast a grateful glance at her cook who gave a disgruntled *harrumph*. "This is Mrs. Wagner, and she's been with us since the boys were born. I couldn't run the ranch without her."

"It's nice to meet you, ma'am," Lance said.

Mrs. Wagner watched him impassively, her steely blue eyes giving him the impression that he had been found lacking. She was a plump woman, with beefy arms and strong hands who appeared to rule her kitchen with ease.

Lance waited for everyone to sit and took the one vacant chair. When they were seated, he helped himself to a generous portion of the pot roast, vegetables, and potato. A basket of bread and a crock of butter were passed around, too.

"You had the boys working with you this afternoon," Zachariah said as he studied Lance. Eleanor sat at the head of the table with her boys on either side of her while Lance sat beside Simon, and Zachariah was across from him and next to Peter. Mrs. Wagner sat at the other end of the table, nearest to the stove, and she hopped up and down frequently to return to the kitchen for more food or to stir something on the stovetop.

Lance speared a roasted carrot with his fork and nodded. "Yes, and they were good helpers. It would have been impossible for me to shore up the bunkhouse roof alone, and I imagine you are too busy to concern yourself with such a trivial task."

Zachariah remained silent as the two men stared at each other for a long moment. "Remember they are boys."

Lance frowned at the warning he heard in Zachariah's tone. "Yes, they are. And they need to learn basic tasks. It does them no good to not know one end of a hammer from the other or to act recklessly around a horse." He gave Simon's shoulder a pat to take away any sting from his words. "Now is the time for them to learn."

Eleanor cleared her throat, and Zachariah lowered his gaze, focusing on his food. "We are appreciative for the work you will do for us, Mr. Gallagher. However, do not allow my boys to become an unnecessary distraction."

"But, Mama," Simon protested as he looked at his mother beseechingly. His black hair was wet from his recent predinner wash, and he wore a clean, light blue shirt that enhanced the color of his eyes. He bit his lip at his mother's stern glower.

"I assure you, ma'am, I will let them know when they have become a distraction." Lance looked down at Simon and winked, earning a grin from the young boy.

CHAPTER 2

The following morning, Lance rose early as was his custom. He dressed and stumbled out to the bunkhouse porch, scratching at his head and silently berating himself for not arranging a way to make coffee for himself. "I'll never make it until 8 a.m.," he muttered. He yawned hugely and stretched his arms over his head, his fingers tracing the low porch ceiling.

He sighed and patted his blond hair that tended to stand on end when he woke each morning. A rooster crowed, a cow gave a mournful moo, and he smiled. "Ranch life," he said with contentment. The underbelly of the clouds shone a soft pink that subtly changed to a hint of purple and then to a darker pink. After a few moments, the brilliant color faded, and the sky brightened. He watched as the light changed, casting bright rays on the distant mountains.

The door to the ranch house opened and closed, and he stared at Mrs. Ferguson approaching him. Her hands were full, and he walked toward her. "May I help you, ma'am?"

She smiled as she held out a cup of coffee. "I feared you were waiting until breakfast. I forgot to inform you a pot of coffee is always on the stove, starting at around six. If you want a cup, you are welcome to come in for one."

He frowned as he studied her. "Don't you lock your doors, Mrs. Ferguson?"

She flushed at the concern in his voice. "We do, but Mrs. Wagner is awake at that time. She unlocks the door as Zachariah likes a cup of coffee early in the morning." She fought a smile. "And his attempts at making his own coffee were disastrous."

Lance chuckled and raised his mug in a small toast. "I thank you." He took a sip and closed his eyes. "Heaven," he whispered.

"Mrs. Wagner is a wonderful cook," Eleanor murmured. She continued to his bunkhouse, carrying a dustpan and broom. "I brought you these.

I fear the bunkhouse is in need of a clean out after months of disuse."

He motioned for her to set them beside the door. "I will do a quick sweep up of the dust. Believe me, after nights of sleep on a bedroll or in questionable establishments, the bunkhouse is akin to paradise."

She stared at him with unveiled curiosity. "Where are you from, Mr. Gallagher? You seem much more … refined than the usual ranch hand."

He shrugged. "I'm from everywhere and nowhere, ma'am. I call no place home." He shrugged. "I was last in Deadwood."

Her eyes bulged. "Deadwood? But that's a wild place." She flushed as she blurted that out.

He chuckled. "Yes, it was. And I found I had no aptitude for gambling or mining." He frowned as he saw her fidget at the mention of gambling.

She cleared her throat. "As long as you understand there is to be no gambling on the Broken Pine."

He nodded. "Like I said, I have no aptitude for it." He frowned as though deep in thought. "Is that why the other hands had trouble remaining here? They wanted to gamble, and you wouldn't allow it?"

She sighed and shook her head. "No. They didn't

like that the orders came from me. Not from Zachariah."

Lance frowned. "Where would they go? Work can't be that plentiful in this area."

"There's more than you'd think. At least four ranches are nearby, and, now that the mines are running again, a few thought they'd become rich looking for the mother lode. They didn't have the sense to realize that there isn't as much demand for silver since the Panic of '73. But, I've learned not to try to reason with men in search of easy riches."

Lance shook his head. "Fools. The only people who become rich are the ones who supply the miners or ply them with drink." He paused as he looked at her with appreciation. "And you are wise not to waste your breath on such men." He scratched at his head as he thought of what she did not say and spoke as the silence grew between them. "Well, I thank you, ma'am, for the coffee and for the broom. I'll bring it back to the main house when it's time for breakfast."

She walked a few paces away and then stopped. "Thank you for being good to my boys. I know they can be a handful."

Lance watched her in confusion. "They were a delight yesterday. I fear they will be disappointed when they learn what chores I have in store for them today." He saw her stiffen. "Never fear, ma'am. I'll never ask them to do anything out of their ability. Although I won't promise not to challenge them. Young boys need to be challenged and to learn that they can succeed."

She relaxed and sighed with relief before nodding her agreement. "Thank you, Mr. Gallagher. I'll see you at breakfast."

He took another deep sip of his coffee and watched her return to the main house. The sun glinted on her hair, enhancing the red in the brown and making her appear younger than she was. He shook his head and forced himself to look to the barn and paddocks and to consider all the work that must be done. He would not be fascinated by the ranch owner.

Later that morning, Lance worked in the barn cleaning out stalls. He had placed the ten ranch horses in the paddocks for now. He clicked to Amaretto and rubbed a hand down his nose before moving him outside, too. After ensuring the water troughs were full, he began the arduous task of mucking out stalls and laying down fresh hay.

The barn was a long, low-roofed building with no storage area over the stalls. A door led to the attached paddock which had a long, narrow covered area where horses could weather any storm or could escape the heat of the day. Inside the barn, a milk cow and two goats occupied two of the stalls.

"Interesting job to do first," Zachariah said as he entered the barn. He looked up at the roof and then to Lance.

Lance leaned on the handle of his shovel and took a deep breath. "I decided if I was to make my horse comfortable, the other animals deserved it, too. I'll get to the roof in a day or two. Winter's a ways off."

Zachariah pulled out another shovel from the storeroom and heaved muck into the wheelbarrow. "I've always thought the barn should be larger, but we've never had time to enlarge it."

Lance looked at the stalls and shrugged. "As long as you don't have too serious a winter, the covered area in the paddock will suffice." He continued his smooth motion of shoveling. "A separate barn for the milk cows and goats might be a good idea, and a covered area for hay out back would be helpful."

Zachariah grabbed the handles of the wheelbarrow. "There are no funds for that right now." After he returned from dumping the load of dirtied straw, he looked at Lance. "You are aware that your pay consists of room and board. Nothing more?"

Lance paused and met the foreman's challenging stare. "I am. It's all I need." He looked around the barn and sighed at the amount of work needed to be done. "You know I'd prefer to be riding Amaretto on the range herding cattle. But I enjoy any work."

Zachariah studied him, crossing his arms over his chest. "Why? Most men who've answered the ad have balked at the menial chores. I thought you'd be upset at missing out on moving the herd to the high mountain pasture for summer." Each year, as the lower valley dried out under the scorching Nevada sun, they moved the herd to a valley high in the mountains that remained lushly green with plenty of grass for the cattle to eat all summer. They would drive the cattle back down to the lower valley in October as winter approached and to cull the herd, sending some of the herd to Chicago to sell.

Lance's eyes brightened for a moment at the prospect of that adventure before he shook his head. "I'll never regret having work." He paused and seemed to consider all that he had learned since his arrival the previous day. "Do you mean those other men were offended at the thought of working for a woman? Or of not playing cowboy?" Lance smiled and shook his head. "I prefer to remain busy, and I realized last night that the work you have for me to do here will keep me much more occupied that watching a grazing herd of cattle."

Zachariah took a step toward him, his blue eyes flashing with concern. "Who are you running from?"

Lance frowned and then half smiled. "I'm in no trouble with the law, and no one is looking for me." He let out a deep breath as he saw his words had not calmed the protective foreman. "Memories. I try to outrun memories." A flash of sorrow shone in his gaze, and then he grabbed his shovel. "This work won't complete itself on its own."

Zachariah grabbed the shovel and shook his head. "I know Mrs. Ferguson hired you, but I can fire you at any moment. I won't allow her or the boys to be harmed."

They glared at each other a long moment before Lance finally wrenched the shovel out of Zachariah's hand. "I have no interest in hurting anyone." He took a deep breath. "I was in Deadwood before I came here. And a few ranches before that." He shrugged. "I know my way around mining towns. I have no desire to be a miner. Besides, I've found that those who make the money are those selling to the miners. I've no interest in setting up a business, and I'd rather be outdoors, outside of town."

The foreman nodded and backed away. "Fine. Don't let harm come to those boys."

Lance glowered at him. "They need to learn about hard work. One of them is at least ten." He paused as Zachariah muttered, "Eleven," and nodded in confirmation. "He should be an accomplished horseman and have a list of chores to do every day. Don't expect me to coddle them when they work with me."

"Good," Zachariah said. "It's what should have occurred years ago, but ..." He broke off as Simon and Peter raced into the barn.

"We're here!" Simon yelled, thrusting his arms wide at their arrival.

Lance laughed and ruffled Simon's black hair. "You are. Go find some shovels, and you can help me muck out stalls." When they made disgusted faces, he gave them a long look. After only a moment, they raced to the cluttered storage room, and he heard them muttering to each other about finding the perfect shovel.

"Good luck with the boys," Zachariah said as he left the barn.

A few days later, Lance worked on the barn roof hammering in nails as he secured new shingles. He swiped his forearm across his brow as he glanced at the roof and shook his head in wonder that the roof hadn't already sprung a leak. Or multiple leaks. Looking over the surrounding land from his high vantage point, he saw willows and cottonwoods in the distance and imagined a creek to be nearby. Few cattle were visible, and he remembered Zachariah saying they had been moved to the higher pastures with lush grass. From what Zachariah had said, he hoped to join his men in the higher country soon.

Lance sighed as he slammed the hammer down again. Although thankful for the work, he longed to ride the land. To feel unfettered again. He gave a disgruntled snort. "You gave up your homestead. You have no right to complain," he muttered to himself. Although he had not lied to Zachariah, and he appreciated being busy, there were moments he yearned to ride as though uninhibited by any obligations. Even the minimal obligations of a ranch hand.

A noise distracted him from his thoughts and made him glance up. He looked toward the road heading to the town of Rattlesnake Ridge and the long drive leading to the ranch. He squinted as a wagon turned up the drive.

Looking down to the ladder propped against the side of the barn, he gave a sharp whistle. Simon poked his head up, as he had volunteered to run for supplies if they were needed. In reality, he sat in the shade and sang to himself while Lance worked on the roof. "Yes, Mr. Lance?" he called out in his excited, youthful voice. He hopped around. "What do I get to do?"

Lance smiled. "Tell your mother that visitors are heading down the lane."

"I'm a sentry!" Simon protested before running to scramble up the half-dead tree behind the bunkhouse to peer down the lane. He gave a whoop of joy and fell nearly head first out of the tree before racing to the house bellowing incoherently to his mother.

Lance chuckled and continued to work, although he cast frequent glances up the lane to see whose arrival warranted such fanfare. As the wagon approached, he saw an attractive, well-dressed woman easily managing the horses pulling her wagon with two children beside her. A pair of dogs paced in the back of the wagon. He smiled at the children when they gaped at him standing on the barn roof as they rolled past before coming to a halt in front of the ranch house.

He heard Eleanor exclaim, "Barb!" and then a cacophony of voices and dogs barking as the guests were welcomed to the ranch. "Work," he muttered to himself. "You're a hired hand."

He slammed the hammer down so hard he nearly shattered the shingle in half. With a sigh, he forced himself to concentrate on his work and fought to ignore the delighted voices below him.

"Barb!" Eleanor exclaimed as she raced from the house and down the front steps. She held her arms open as she waited for Zachariah to help Barb and her children out of the wagon. Eleanor pulled her close, squeezing her tight. "Oh, it's so wonderful to see you! I had no idea you were planning a visit today."

"Jack encouraged us to visit. Thought we needed

a day away from the house." Barbara's husband was Jack Hollis, Deputy Sheriff of Rattlesnake Ridge. She released Eleanor and wrapped an arm around each of her twin children's shoulders. "He thought Ishmael and Isabelle could use a little time running around the ranch, playing with your boys. I think Jack hopes they'll return home exhausted." The two friends shared a smile.

Eleanor pulled the two children close and kissed their foreheads. "I know Peter and Simon will enjoy any excuse to play." She watched as the four children and the two dogs ran off together. "Simon will try hard to keep up," she murmured as she saw her six-year-old struggle to run as fast as the thirteen-year-old twins and his eleven-year-old brother.

"And Isabelle will have to convince them that a girl still enjoys playing in the mud and finding frogs," Barbara said with a chuckle. "Come, let's enjoy our time free of children." She looped her arm through Eleanor's, and they ascended the steps to the ranch house porch.

Zachariah returned to the barn, leaving the women alone.

Barbara watched his departure from the porch and raised an eyebrow. "He's as attentive as ever," she murmured.

"Don't start," Eleanor said with a sigh. "You know we've only ever been good friends." She frowned when her best friend made a face and looked embarrassed. "Barb?"

Barbara ran a hand over the skirt of her blue calico dress that enhanced her natural curves and the beauty of her blonde hair. "I ... I don't know how to tell you what is being whispered about you in town."

Eleanor tugged her to a pair of rocking chairs, and they sat down. A pitcher of water with glasses sat on a table between the chairs. "I know they continue to whisper about the disgrace of my husband's death. And they remain dumbfounded that I manage the ranch."

Barbara flushed beet red, and her eyes lit with anger. "That's just it, Eleanor. Someone, and I'm not sure who, started the rumor that the reason the bank hasn't had to take over the ranch is because Zachariah is really running it."

Eleanor looked at her friend with a puzzled expression. "That comes as no surprise to me, Barb. Why should that upset you? Few men believe a woman capable of managing such an enterprise. Never mind helping it to thrive." She grimaced. "Except for last year when the price of cattle sank."

"Well, there's more to it. It seems that there are those who believe Alan intentionally sought death at that card table. Because he was tired of living a lie." She gripped Eleanor's hand as Eleanor paled.

"What? I don't understand." A tear tracked down Eleanor's cheek. "I know the last few years of our marriage were difficult. He never took to being a father and resented the time the boys wanted to spend with him. Hated the time I spent with the children, called me doting and smothering. He was bitter at the help I provided to keep the ranch running, and was annoyed at the partnership Zachariah and I forged to keep the ranch running smoothly." She sniffled.

Barbara let out a deep breath. "I never realized it was that difficult."

Eleanor shrugged. "Then, suddenly I was a widow, due to my husband's proclivity to gamble, and I was expected to mourn and wail and show remorse. And I was sad, Barb. I promise I was. But I also felt a tremendous guilt." She closed her eyes and let out a deep breath. "Such guilt because I felt relief that all that strife had come to an end. That my worst fear hadn't come true."

When Eleanor remained silent, Barb whispered, "What was that?"

Eleanor opened guilt-stricken eyes. "That he'd gambled away our ranch and left me destitute. He talked about doing it on a nearly weekly basis." Her eyes shone with anger as she recalled those conversations. "That we'd lose everything due to his..." She let out a deep breath. "I felt such relief to know that could never come true."

"Oh, Eleanor," Barbara whispered.

Eleanor's eyes were shiny with unshed tears. "A few harsh words here and there by the townsfolk will never be worse than what I say to myself. For I did not mourn as a loving, grieving widow should. And that is what shames me."

Barbara bit her lip and then murmured, "It is said that the reason Alan never took to the boys, especially to Simon, is because Simon wasn't—isn't —his."

Eleanor's eyes widened with shock, and she gaped at Barbara. "I beg your pardon? Who would suggest such a... scandalous... horrible thing?"

Barbara shrugged. "Those who like to gossip. And they thrive on it."

Eleanor rubbed at her forehead. "This is why I was treated in town differently the last few times I've gone in for supplies. This is why I've had fewer visitors," she whispered. "I swear to you, Barb, I was always true to my vows. I never..." Her voice broke. "I would never do what they are suggesting."

Barbara nodded. "I know. It's why I was so angry. And it's why I made a point of telling everyone in the General Store today that I was heading here to see you with my children and that Jack had encouraged me to visit. A few were shocked, but more looked chagrined that they had given any credence to the rumors."

"How do you fight such... nastiness?" Eleanor whispered as she swiped at her cheek.

"You can't," Barbara said as she squeezed Eleanor's hand. "You must hold your head high and continue to be the respectable woman you are known to be."

After a long moment, where Eleanor looked toward the barn, she whispered, "They think it's Zachariah, don't they?" She shook her head ruefully. "Why is it that the townsfolk can't understand a friendship between a man and a woman?"

"Because it's rarer than a raincloud in July in these parts," Barbara said with a wry smile. "They can't understand it because they are incapable of it. However, I wouldn't let their nasty speculation ruin the friendship you do have, Eleanor."

Eleanor sighed. "I shouldn't be surprised. I knew

there would be someone who would make an offensive comment when Simon was born with black hair. No one ever bothers to learn that my mother had black hair. Blacker than Simon's." She looked in the direction her youngest son had run off to play and smiled. "He reminds me of her."

Barbara nodded. "If they bothered to look closely, they'd also see he has Alan's smile and Alan's spirit."

Eleanor shivered. "My hope is that Simon has Alan's curiosity but not his recklessness." She swiped at her cheeks.

"You mustn't be afraid of him being a boy and exploring the world around him," Barbara soothed. "He will do reckless things, but that is normal. You mustn't always imagine it is due to him being Alan's son."

"It's so hard," she whispered. "I dread anything happening to him or to Peter. I don't know what I would do."

Barbara nodded. "I know. But I also know that trying to protect them from every mishap will only hurt them in the long run."

Eleanor closed her eyes for a moment before she changed the subject. "I must admit, this new gossip makes going into town for Sunday service less enticing." She shared a rueful smile with her friend.

"But you must go, Eleanor," Barbara urged.

"Yes, I know. I must." She was silent a long moment. "What was it like for you, overcoming their gossip because you sang and played the piano in the saloon?"

Barbara flushed at the mention of what she did after her first husband had died, and she had to find a way to earn a living to support herself and her twins. "It was challenging at times, but I soon had the support of Mrs. Brown." She smiled. "That woman is not to be crossed. If she hears of the comments disparaging you, I have a feeling she will find a way to make those gossipers atone."

Eleanor smiled with satisfaction as she thought about the reverend's wife. "She is a force to be reckoned with, isn't she?"

Barbara giggled. "Yes. Even the most rough-and-tumble miner doesn't dare cross her. That's why it's vital for you to go to church on Sunday. She will have a greater chance of hearing the murmurings if you are there. Too many of the gossips can't help sharing what they've heard, and their voices are louder than they think."

Eleanor sighed. "I think it will be important my

new ranch hand accompany us." She nodded to the man working diligently on her barn roof. "His presence here should dispel the notion that working for a woman is a challenge."

Barbara squinted as she looked at Lance kneeling on the roof, the muscles under his shirt rippling as he hammered in nails. "He sure is fine to look at. Are you certain you can trust having him here on the ranch?"

Eleanor shrugged. "I fear I don't have a lot of choice. We need help." She spread her arms as though to encompass the ranch falling apart, board by board, around her. "He knows what needs to be done and does it." She met her friend's worried gaze. "And he ran to the paddock to protect Simon within the first five minutes of arriving here. Calmed Spirit when Simon tried to bring him into the paddock alone."

Barbara gasped. "Spirit's barely tamed."

"I know. But Mr. Gallagher approached him and had Spirit nuzzling against his chest in a matter of moments. I've never seen the like." A mischievous smile spread. "I think Zachariah was a bit jealous, as Spirit has only ever snorted and misbehaved for him."

Barbara let out a deep breath and looked with a

mother's appreciation at the man working on the roof. "Thank heavens he knew what to do."

Eleanor smiled. "Yes. And since then, he's been good to both boys. Encouraging them to work with him, but ensuring the tasks are within their abilities." She blinked away tears. "I never realized how much they were missing a male presence in their life. They have Zachariah, but he tends to keep himself separate." She sniffled. "With Mr. Gallagher, they follow him around like a puppy, and he doesn't seem to mind."

Barbara took a deep sip of water. "Well, hopefully he will prove worthy of the trust you have already bestowed upon him."

Eleanor looked at Lance as she nodded. "Yes, I hope so."

CHAPTER 3

"**B**oys!" Eleanor called up the stairs. She waited a moment, and, when she failed to hear a responding thud to her call, she yelled again. "Boys! It's time to leave. You'll have no dessert if we're late to service." She waited with a smile as she heard shouts of distress and two pairs of feet scampering around above her as they raced for the stairs.

"Mama! We're ready," Peter said as he sailed down the stairs. His shirt was only half tucked in, and one shoe was untied. She motioned for him to make himself presentable for church and focused on her youngest.

Simon looked as though he'd just wrestled with a hedgehog and lost. His hair was on end, his previously pristine white shirt had a red splotch on the chest, and his trousers had a tear at the knee.

"Oh, Simon," she whispered as she fought a chuckle. "What did you do?"

He held up his arms, only one arm in his good coat for church. "It doesn't fit well, Mama."

She looked at him with a critical eye and nodded. "You're right. You're getting too big for your jacket, and we don't have time to adjust one of Peter's. For now, you'll make do." She looked at him with confusion. "I was upstairs not ten minutes ago, and your clothes were fine. What happened?"

He shrugged. "I thought I saw a mouse and tried to trap it. Instead, I caught the nail on my pail lunchbox and then scratched my finger." He held up his left index finger that showed little sign of injury and waited for his mother to react.

She smiled as she leaned forward and kissed it. "And then what happened, my little love?"

He thrust his arm out with excitement, thwacking the wall with the free arm of his jacket. "And then the mouse jumped back out again, and we had to chase it around. But it got away." He ducked his head as though that were a shame.

"They tend to outsmart us humans," she said with an affectionate smile. "Come, we don't have time to put you to rights before church." She attempted to tame his wild hair with a few pats, and then helped him on with his jacket. She frowned when she saw him in it. "This fits you perfectly, Simon."

He pulled at the sleeve of it. "I don't like it, Mama."

"Just because you don't like something, Simon, doesn't mean you should tell me a fib. It would have cost me money we shouldn't spend on buying fabric you don't need." She waited until he nodded his head in understanding. "Come, boys."

They departed their house to find Zachariah and Lance waiting for them. Lance grabbed Simon while Zachariah grabbed Peter, hauling the boys into the back of the wagon. Lance rode his horse, Amaretto, while Eleanor rode beside Zachariah in the wagon.

"Mr. Lance!" Simon called out as they made their way to town. "Mr. Lance, did you know we have a mouse in the house?" He giggled as the sentence rhymed.

Lance shook his head. "No, but that's quite common. They like to be near little boys."

Peter and Simon shared confused looks and then looked at Lance. "Why?"

"Because little boys often hide food and other treats in their bedrooms. They know they can nibble on those treats when the boys aren't looking." He laughed as the brothers made gagging noises.

"Of course you boys would never do such a thing, would you?" Eleanor said as she looked back at her sons. "It is strictly forbidden to have food on the second floor."

Simon opened his mouth and then hung his head. "I already fibbed once today, Mama. I can't tell another one, or the preacher won't let me in the church." He met his mother's patient stare. "We keep a little cheese and bread in our bedside drawer."

"And why would you do that?" Zachariah asked.

"We're always hungry, and Mrs. Wagner says we eat too much. When we ask her for snacks, she slaps our hands and tells us we are *guillotines* and that it's our greatest sin," Peter said.

"What does that mean, Mama?" Simon asked.

Lance chuckled. "Gluttonous, Peter. It means you eat more than you should. But you're growing boys, and you'll eat a lot more before you're through."

Eleanor sighed. "I'll speak with her. I'd much rather have you eat a midnight snack in the kitchen than in your bedrooms. I do not like mice being upstairs." She shivered at the thought.

As they continued the journey to town, the rolling hills became more barren as they left the foothills of the mountains behind. Soon, few trees were visible, and the bright blue sky was a stark contrast to the burnt brown of the land. A hawk flew overhead, swooping and soaring as it searched for prey.

A short time later, the wagon rattled into the town of Rattlesnake Ridge. What had once been little more than a blip on a map was now a growing, prosperous town due to the productive silver mines. Although not as profitable as they would have been before the Panic of 1873 and the US government's move to the gold standard due to the Coinage Act of 1873, a market remained for the silver mined in the hills. The town was set at the base of the hills, with the mines above, and there was little relief from the harsh Nevada environment. Few trees were visible from town as they had been cut long ago for lumber for support beams in the mines. The mines scarred many of the hills and filled the town with dirt and soot. The overwhelming bleakness astonished Lance once again as he rode beside the wagon. He gave silent thanks that he had found work on a ranch outside of town.

As they made their way through town, they passed the office of the town paper, the *Rattlesnake Ridge Recorder*, and the bank. Zachariah paused at the intersection of Main Street, waiting for a wagonful of lumber to roll past before he steered the horses to the nearby church. The streets were busy with commerce and residents traveling to hear the weekly sermon.

Eleanor turned around and looked at her sons. Already numerous wagons were in the open space near the church. "I don't want any more calamities occurring to your Sunday-best clothes, boys. Behave today."

"Yes, Mama," they parroted at the same time as their shoulders slumped. However, their spirits quickly rose when they saw friends arriving with their parents.

"There's Isabelle and Ishmael!" Simon said and yelled his hello as he waved. He toppled over as the wagon lurched to a halt but pushed himself up to see if his friends were still in sight.

"They've gone in, Simon," Lance said as he dismounted Amaretto and tied him to a post next to their wagon. "Rub the dirt off your jacket and pants before your mother sees it." He winked at Simon as the boy patted at himself to rid the dirt from his mother's notice.

Lance hauled the boys down from the back of the wagon so their clothes would remain cleaner and waited as Zachariah helped Eleanor down. Lance walked a pace behind the family as they approached the church, watching as they were warmly welcomed by all who loitered outside before the day's sermon. He nodded to those who stared at him with curiosity, and watched as Simon and Peter bristled with pent-up energy to run and play with boys their own age. However, they soon entered the too-hot church to hear the reverend's sermon.

L ance stood outside after the service and took a deep breath of the relatively cooler air. The church had been stifling with the mass of bodies pressed together on the warm summer day. He nodded in a friendly, but noncommittal manner to others leaving the church. He had no desire to strike up a meaningless conversation. Instead, he stood to one side of the church as Eleanor spoke with friends, and Zachariah stood on the opposite side of the church talking with other ranchers. The boys raced around, playing with their friends while attempting not to dirty their Sunday-best clothes. Lance smiled as he watched Simon trying to keep up with Ishmael and Peter and knew it was a matter of time before they ended up in a pile of something that would offend their mothers.

The warm July sun beat down, and Lance moved farther into the building's shadow, leaning against the whitewashed wall. Wagons rattled by, and the sound of men hammering in the nearby hills could be heard as a new mine was dug and the walls shored up with freshly cut lumber from the nearby sawmill. Mine tailings formed small hills near the entrances to the mines. There was little beauty in the town in summertime with the landscape parched dry.

As he leaned against the wall, he puzzled through Eleanor's reaction to the reverend's impassioned sermon about the perils of gossiping. Why had she been uncomfortable, and why did many of the townswomen glance in her direction? He set aside his concerns and watched Zachariah's approach. Lance stood tall, nodding to the man next to his boss.

"This is Lance Gallagher," Zachariah said to the man next to him. "He's our new hand. Has a way with horses, but lately he's been busy with a hammer as he makes repairs so the place doesn't fall apart around us."

Lance looked up to meet the inquisitive gaze of

one of the tallest men he'd ever met. The man had a scar along his chin which caused his welcoming smile to appear crooked. "Nice to meet you," Lance said with a nod.

"I'm Jack Hollis, the deputy," Jack said as he stared intently at Lance. He seemed to be taking Lance's measure after mentioning he was a man of the law, and, when Lance failed to bristle, he relaxed subtly. "It's a relief to hear Mrs. Ferguson has hired a competent hand willing to do more than ride around chasing cattle."

"I do what I'm asked to," Lance murmured.

"My wife, Barb, and our children were at the ranch last week. I think you saw them." At Lance's nod of agreement, Jack said, "She was impressed with all the work you'd managed to get done in the short time you'd been there."

"Sometimes all you need is another set of hands to turn things around," Lance said. "I know how hard it can be to run a ranch with limited help."

Zachariah tipped his wide-brimmed black hat back on his forehead and looked at Lance with curiosity. "Do you? I've never been able to figure out much about what you did before you arrived at our ranch."

Lance looked at the two men with wary concern

as though belatedly understanding they had subtly cornered him. "I believe there's little use in focusing on the past when all we have is the here and now. I drifted about, and I've seen my share of the country. As I told you, the last place I called home before Rattlesnake Ridge was Deadwood."

Jack looked at him and crossed his arms over his strong chest. "Did you fight in the War?"

Lance nodded. "Yes. In the Union Cavalry." He watched the deputy calm at the mention of fighting for the Union. Although a decade had passed since the Civil War had ended, he understood that some wounds took years to heal.

"That's why you're so good with horses," Zachariah said.

"I've been around them since I was a boy, and I've always had a way with them. Anyone who mistreats their horse is a fool."

"That he is," Jack said. "Come, you should meet Reverend Brown."

Lance stiffened. "Coming to church was one thing..." he protested as the two men corralled him in the direction of the reverend standing near the church steps.

"Reverend Brown!" Jack called out with a friendly wave. "Wonderful service."

"Aye, I thought a wee sermon about gossip a timely message." He smiled as Zachariah glowered, and Jack nodded. The reverend spoke with a soft Scottish burr in his voice and a welcoming glint in his brown eyes. He stood with his hands over his slight paunch, and he looked as though he could burst into a rendition of a Scottish folk tale at any moment. However, his gaze focused on Lance, and he nodded in welcome. "Hello, young man. I'm certain your help is appreciated at the Ferguson ranch."

Lance held his hat between his fingers, tracing its rim and fighting the urge to fidget under the reverend's inquisitive stare. "I believe it is."

"'Tis good for the townsfolk to see the ranch begin to prosper again. It's been long enough since Mr. Ferguson departed this earth." He bowed his head, as though in honor of his memory a moment, and then patted Lance on his arm. "Come to tea someday." He wandered down the steps to converse with the women watching their children.

Lance sighed and put his hat on. "He isn't serious, is he?"

Zachariah shrugged, frowning as he saw the panicked look in Lance's gaze. "Yes. When he asks you for tea, it means he wants you to visit soon. I'm sure you'll have a formal invitation within the next week."

"And don't even consider missing your time with him," Jack said in his deep voice. "He'll just hunt you down and force you to talk with him."

Zachariah shivered. "Believe me, that's worse."

Lance sighed again, muttering, "Meddlesome preacher," and glared at the two men as they chuckled. His gaze focused on Eleanor as he saw her speaking with Barbara before walking into town.

Zachariah followed his gaze and shook his head in resignation. "She's the most mule-headed woman you'll ever meet." After a moment, he murmured, "But the strongest, too. She won't let a little gossip prevent her from going to the General Store."

"You'll never know how thankful I am that Barb does the shopping there now. I always hated Mrs. Handley's meddling." He, too, watched as Eleanor strolled down the street, greeting all she passed. "Mrs. Ferguson's always been brave."

Lance frowned at the men as they discussed Eleanor without offering any insight into the subject everyone in town seemed to understand except him. As Eleanor turned down Main Street in the direction of the General Store, he fought an urge to race after her so as to protect her from an unknown foe.

Eleanor walked the short distance from the church on the outskirts of town to the large mercantile closer to the center of town. Barbara had agreed to watch her boys while she placed an order for supplies at the store. She smiled to the townsfolk she passed and ignored the inquisitive stare from Mr. Langhorne, the town reporter, as he lounged against the doorjamb of the saloon across the street. Although a friendly, energetic man, she knew he was always eager to find an interesting story to report. She had no desire for her family to appear as a frequent topic in his publication.

The bell of the General Store rang as she opened the door, and she squared her shoulders and pasted on a friendly smile as she entered the Handleys' establishment. The subtle fragrances of licorice, coffee, and soap mixed together to form a miasma of scents. Bright sunlight entered the front windows on either side of the door, and the lower windows were open as the day warmed further. Bins filled with spices and foodstuffs lined one side of the store, while items for the home or ranch lined the other wall.

After glancing wistfully at the fabric display,

Eleanor forced herself to ignore it and to focus on the necessities needed at the ranch. She gripped the list she and Mrs. Wagner had made and approached Mrs. Handley. Eleanor's smile dimmed as she saw the mischievous intent in the storeowner's gaze. "Good day, Mrs. Handley. I have a list of items we need at the ranch." She set her list on the countertop.

Mrs. Handley smiled at her but did not reach for the list. "How wonderful to see you in town again, Mrs. Ferguson. I imagine it has been quite a trial for you, all alone on your ranch these many months. As you can imagine, we've been quite worried about you."

Eleanor stood straight, her smile rigid and devoid of warmth. "If you were truly concerned, Mrs. Handley, you could have visited me at the ranch. You would have been quite welcome."

Mrs. Handley laughed and ran a hand over her indigo blue dress. "I'm much too busy for such social calls." She reached forward and tapped Eleanor on her arm. "But never fear, dear, I've been kept abreast of your situation by Mr. Hayden. He is most concerned about the state of your ranch. It seems it is on the verge of collapsing about your ears any day now!"

Eleanor bristled. "We've had a difficult time

keeping qualified help willing to do the work required. I'm sure you will be relieved to learn a new man is working on the ranch who is quite adept at all that needs to be done."

Mrs. Handley chuckled and shook her head. "Well, let's hope he stays on the good side of Zachariah. We know why the previous hands left, and it had nothing to do with competence." She raised her eyebrows in expectation of Eleanor's agreement and then frowned as Eleanor glowered at her.

"Mr. O'Neill is a trusted friend, a hard worker, and an excellent foreman. There should be no doubt as to his judgment regarding the competence of a ranch hand." Eleanor glared at Mrs. Handley and sighed as she realized a small crowd of women had gathered behind her as she spoke with the shop-keeper. "If you would be so kind as to fill this order, we will return as we leave town."

Eleanor waited for Mrs. Handley to reach for her list and then nodded to the meddlesome woman. She turned away from the front of the store and smiled at the town's women who now avidly studied china patterns or debated the merits of tea over coffee. When she stood outside again, Eleanor breathed a sigh of relief before returning to the church to collect her family.

T hat evening, Eleanor sat on the front porch after her boys had gone to bed. She'd read three bedtime stories to Simon before he finally settled. She smiled as she thought about her spirited boy.

"It's good to see you pleased about something," Zachariah said as he climbed the porch steps after walking over from his small foreman's cabin. "You were too quiet after coming back from town."

She looked at her friend and flushed. "I had my reasons." When he looked at her in confusion, she shrugged. "What's the matter, Zachariah?"

He sat with an appreciative groan in the chair next to her and stretched out his legs. "I want to head to the upper pasture. To ensure that all is well with our herd."

She frowned at the fine tension that seemed to thrum through him. "What aren't you telling me?"

He looked at her and met her concerned gaze. "Nothing. I promised you after Alan died that I would always be honest. That I would never keep secrets about the ranch from you. And I haven't. There's no reason for me to be worried." He looked to the mountains in the distance again.

She whispered, "But you are."

He nodded. "Yeah. I have this feeling something's not right. That something bad is going to happen. I spoke with Jack about it, but he assures me there is no reason for concern. He's heard of nothing nefarious occurring. But I worry he's missed something." He gripped her hand when she gasped in dismay. "It doesn't mean something bad will happen, El."

She blinked away tears. "It feels like, no matter how hard we work, we're doomed to fail."

He squeezed her hand and chuckled. "No need to be dramatic. We aren't failing. We're a long way from failing." He took a deep breath as he looked at her. "You pay the loan on time, and there's money in the bank in case the cattle prices remain low."

She nodded. "Yes," she whispered. "I hate worrying about what might happen if prices remain depressed like last year."

"That's why you have savings, El." Zachariah attempted to give her a reassuring smile, but his bolstering smile did little to alleviate her worry as she hugged her arms more tightly about her middle.

"I'd far prefer to use them to pay my foreman and

ranch hands more than room and board." She looked in the direction of the barn. "And to continue to have money set aside in case of a true emergency."

"Not paying the bank loan is an emergency. You don't pay that loan, you won't have a ranch." Zachariah bit back an oath as he saw her flinch as his tone was harsher than he intended. "El, I'm sorry."

"No," she murmured. "You're honest. And I've always wanted honesty from you, Zachariah." She reached out and squeezed his arm. "It's why you're my best friend."

He nodded. "Although that's only brought you trouble." He frowned as she stood, lowered her head and hand, and stepped away from him. "El, even I know what that sermon was about today."

"How mortifying," she breathed. "I can't imagine …"

He fought a smile as he stared at her. "You can't imagine being more than my friend? It's mortifying considering a relationship with a man who's your brother in every possible way?"

She smiled and relaxed. "Yes. I hate that they continue to find a way to hurt me with their vicious words and innuendoes."

He shrugged. "Their words only have power if

you give it to them. You and I know the truth, El. We know that Simon is Alan's."

"They know the truth, too, if they bothered to pay attention," she said in a disgruntled voice.

He laughed. "Yes, but it will be all the sweeter when those women are forced to eat crow." He winked at her. "I look forward to watching them choke out an apology."

She ran her hands over her arms. "I doubt they will."

"Oh, if Reverend Brown has anything to do with it, they will." He laughed. "And if he doesn't, his wife will ensure they do. No one trifles with Adeline Brown."

She giggled. "No, no one would dare." They stood in companionable silence for a few moments as a cool breeze blew.

"Will you and the boys be all right if I'm away for a few weeks? Even a month?" Zachariah asked in a low voice.

"I'll miss you, Zachariah. And I'll hate not having you here for Sterling's visits," she whispered as she sniffled. "But you must ensure the cattle are well tended. If we don't have cattle, we don't have a ranch."

"There's the Eleanor I know. The fighter," he said

with admiration. "I'll speak with Lance tomorrow before I leave. I feel better leaving knowing he is here." When she frowned, Zachariah said, "You already trust him with your boys, El. You'll have to trust that he'll work to keep you safe if need be."

She shivered at his words and nodded.

The following morning, Zachariah strode into the barn and gave an appreciative sigh. Rather than the haphazard and failed attempt at order, Lance had cleaned and tidied the barn in a short period of time. Fresh hay lined each stall, and the horses stared at Zachariah as though they were more content in their current situation than before. He ran a finger over the muzzle of his favorite horse, Rogue, and turned as Lance entered the barn.

"I'm glad you're here," Zachariah said. "I know you haven't been on the ranch long, but you've already earned our trust. You are patient with the boys, and you never appear annoyed when they insist on aiding you with your work. In fact, you seem to take great pleasure in the time you spend with them."

Lance nodded and watched Zachariah guardedly.

He patted Amaretto as he butted his head upward in hopes of receiving a treat.

"I must travel to the summer pastures. I want to check on our cattle and ensure everything is well." His gaze was distant as though envisioning the green pastures in the high mountain valleys, the cowboys watching over the herd and Cookie in his wagon.

"How is it you have more land than the 160 acres in a normal homestead?" Lance asked. "If your land extends to the mountains, it would be much larger than the single tract granted in the usual land grant."

Zachariah sighed and leaned against one of the stall doors. "Alan Ferguson and I were friends since we were young. Made it through the War together. The dream of what we'd do if we survived the War kept us going through…" His voice faded as his gaze dulled as though envisioning distant battle scenes. He shook his head. "We dreamed of coming West, of escaping the memories of that conflict." He saw the echo of similar memories in Lance's gaze and nodded. "After surviving the War, he married his sweetheart, Eleanor. And the three of us wandered."

Zachariah sighed. "It was a horrible life for a man, but even worse for a woman who by now had a child. Alan always had the dream of the next successful ploy for money or a business. But he was a horrible businessman and even worse with money. He resented that I would find stable work wherever we landed to keep the four of us afloat." He shook his head. "And then one night, after we found lodging at Miz May's boarding house in Rattlesnake Ridge, he came home, having won at cards."

His gaze was one of dazed amusement. "Alan never won at cards. He never won at anything. But that night, he'd managed to win a ranch—640 acres." He motioned with his hand as though to encompass everything around him. "And we moved here."

Lance frowned. "What about the people living on the ranch at the time?"

"That was a major headache, but Alan had won the ranch fair and square. We kept many of the hands in the beginning and slowly learned ranching. Eleanor had an instinctual aptitude for it, where Alan never took to it." Zachariah paused for a moment.

His frown deepened, and Lance studied Zachariah. "There's more you aren't telling me."

"Of course there is," he said with a smile. "But that's how we came to be at this ranch. Been here seven years now." He stood tall and walked to his horse's stall. "And now I have to head to the summer pasture to ensure all is well."

Lance studied him. "I would have thought your men would send word if they were having trouble."

Zachariah gave a grunt of agreement. "Normally, I would agree with you. However, I worry that they are not as loyal as they should be." He watched Lance frown. "Too many are swayed by the promise of an easy dollar."

"Stealing cattle is no small offense," Lance murmured. "If that is what you imply."

Zachariah rolled his shoulders. "I hope I'm wrong. But I fear for rustlers. And I regret that one of our neighbors is not as ... upstanding as I would wish." He shared a long look with Lance. "Keep a close eye on the boys. And on Mrs. Ferguson. When she has a caller, and she will, please ensure she is not forced to suffer his company for any extended period of time."

"How will I know he is unwelcome?" Lance asked.

Zachariah laughed. "Oh, you'll know the minute he arrives that Mrs. Ferguson wishes him gone. It's only because he has an ego the size of Reno that he doesn't realize it."

CHAPTER 4

Lance worked to shore up the roof covering part of the paddock. He whistled as he sawed logs, hammered them in place, and reinforced the support beams. Soon, he'd work on the roof to ensure the shingles were sound. However, at the moment he was uncertain the roof would handle any extra weight. Thus, he worked to strengthen the main structure. He knew after a few more days of hard work that the paddock area would be secure for winter. Glancing at the ranch house, he frowned as his two young helpers had yet to make an appearance.

While he worked, he thought about the time he had spent on the ranch. A month had passed since his arrival, and Zachariah had already been away two weeks. Lance was on the verge of completing the most immediate work, but plenty remained to be done. Shutters on the ranch house needed to be oiled or have hinges replaced, and he'd noticed Miss Eleanor stepping cautiously on the porch. He suspected a board or two had rotted and needed to be replaced.

He shook his head and silently berated himself for calling her Miss Eleanor. "She's Mrs. Ferguson," he muttered to himself and then bit back a curse as the hammer struck his thumb. He hoped the momentary pain would rid him of his fascination for the ranch owner.

He sighed as he picked up a piece of lumber to saw. The more time he spent in her presence, the more she intrigued him. She was composed, and he would have thought her cold-hearted had he not seen her interact with her boys. With them, she was warm, frequently smiling and laughing. He frowned as he tried to imagine the difficulties and prejudices she had faced running the ranch since her husband had died.

Lance kicked at a dried piece of dung and swore under his breath as he continued to think about his boss. He rubbed at his neck as he admitted the truth: Eleanor fascinated him. Her strength melded with delicate moments of indecision. Her severe posture as she gave him his instructions for the day each morning contrasted with her beautiful reddish-brown hair falling out of its bun. Her attempt at always appearing meek and biddable when the pompous Mr. Hayden visited, the façade betrayed by the intelligent dislike shining in her eyes. "Oh, you're in trouble lad," he muttered to himself.

He looked over his shoulder as the screen door slammed shut to see the object of his musing standing ramrod straight as she stared down the lane. Lance knew it meant Sterling Hayden was making another call. Lance said a silent prayer that he'd have a reason to cut the day's visit short to spare Miss Eleanor the discomfort of Mr. Hayden's presence.

Eleanor stood on the porch as she waited for Sterling Hayden to make his long ride down her driveway. She sighed with irritation at his regular visits and thought uncharitably that he took his time in an effort to preen and show himself in his best light. "There is no good light for him," she muttered as she watched him approach her wearing a smug, overbearing smile. A fine sheen of dust covered his fancy brown suit with silver buttons.

She crossed her hands over each other at her waist and stood tall in her clean, sky blue calico dress that highlighted the beauty of her blue eyes. Rather than any trepidation, annoyance thrummed through her. When he walked up her steps, she battled a grimace to realize he meant to stay for a prolonged visit. "Mr. Hayden," she murmured in a deferential tone. "It is always a pleasure to see you." She moved adroitly to the chairs on the porch, preventing him from grasping her hand and attempting to kiss the back of it. After she had settled her skirts, she waited for him to sit. "I fear in this heat, I only have water to offer you."

"That is all I need after such a journey," he said. He took a long sip of water and grimaced. "Although I do wish you had an ice house."

She shrugged. "Ice is not wasted on cooling water at Broken Pine Ranch, Mr. Hayden." She sat with perfect posture as she waited for him to speak.

He looked at her barn and paddocks and frowned

at the subtle improvements that had occurred since his last visit. The roof had new shingles. Boards that had been on the verge of falling off had been hammered into place or replaced. The long roof of the stalls lining the paddock no longer sagged. "I didn't know Zachariah had that much time to work on the barn," he said with a frown.

She shook her head. "Mr. O'Neill is busy as the foreman overseeing the cattle and spends most of his day on the range." She gave Mr. Hayden a steady, searching look. "As I'm sure you know. He informed me that he spoke with a few of your hands recently who wandered into our summer pasture." Last week, Zachariah had returned for a half-day visit to ensure all was well before returning to the high mountain pasture. However, if Sterling Hayden remained unaware that Zachariah was away from the home-stead, Eleanor had no interest in enlightening him.

Hayden shrugged. "I had sent them to look for cattle that had strayed from the herd."

"Seems an odd coincidence your hands would find their way to where my cattle fatten up for the summer. Few lose their bearings so badly as to wander through a mountain pass into that patch of meadow." She held his gaze, hers challenging with barely a hint of friendliness mixed within. "I'm thankful my men are well trained enough to have marked all of our cattle with our distinctive brand."

"What can I say about a pair of greenhorns?" he said with a chuckle and another shrug.

She smiled although no pleasure reached her eyes. "Yes, I understand all about the difficulty of finding hardworking men willing to work on a ranch." She looked out at her land. "Especially when so few men are willing to work for a woman."

Sterling sighed as he stretched his legs out in front of him, relaxing into his chair. "That's why rarely any widows are successful ranchers. I'm sure your husband wouldn't want you to risk losing all this." He waved at the land in front of them. "This is your sons' birthright."

She nodded. "I agree. It is their birthright. It's why I fight so hard to maintain it for them." She nodded as a figure emerged into the paddock. "I'm thankful a hardworking, experienced hand signed on last month. Had you been at church recently, you would have met him." Her smile was genuine as she watched him attempt to conceal his rage at her hiring help.

"How … fortuitous for you," he muttered.

"Yes. Mr. Langhorne's advertisement was

successful this time." She looked at Sterling Hayden with innocent optimism. "Rather than vagabonds and rogues, I seem to have found a genuine worker."

"I'd be cautious before trusting a stranger, Mrs. Ferguson. For all you know, he's a gambler or worse," he said, his gaze calculating as he saw her flinch subtly at the mention of gambling. "You can never be too careful where your children are concerned."

She cleared her throat. "Of course I know that." She bristled at his insinuation that she was unable to protect her boys. "However, if the work is not done, the ranch will fail. And I will not allow that."

"May I speak plainly?" he asked. Rather than wait for her agreement, he barreled on as he gripped one of her hands. "You know I desire a union between us. That should come as no surprise to you. All you need do is ask, and five able-bodied men will be here to complete whatever task you desire."

She flushed and shook her head. "I... thank you for such consideration, Mr. Hayden." She tugged on her hand but was unable to free it. "I'm not ready."

"It's been two years, Eleanor." He flushed, either from his harsh tone or the use of her first name. He softened his tone as though attempting to woo her to his way of thinking. "Many widows remarry in a matter of months."

"I'm not desperate," she snapped as she yanked her hand away and clasped them together again on her lap. She took a deep breath and met his angry gaze.

"So I'm only good enough if you're desperate?" he asked.

She shook her head. "I never said that, nor did I mean it. However, no woman likes knowing that the only reason she is being wooed is because her land is valued. Not her."

He leaned forward so that his elbows rested on his knees and stared at her frankly. "For months, you've led me on a song-and-dance act, behaving as though you were a meek woman." He shook his head. "You're cold-hearted with a spine of steel, aren't you?" When she remained silent, he dipped his head and whispered, "I want this ranch. I want this land." After a long pause, "And I will have it. You'd do well to remember I always get what I want."

She stood, and he followed suit. "Thank you for such scintillating conversation," she murmured. "I'm certain you've given me quite a bit to consider."

He leaned forward, his coffee- and tobacco-tinged breath wafting over her. "Don't imagine you can thwart me in this, Eleanor."

She glared at him as he marched away, his spurs clanging with each step. After he mounted his horse and rode away at a canter, she collapsed into her chair. She held her hands together to prevent them from shaking and jolted at the soft voice coming from the other side of the railing.

"Are you all right, Mrs. Ferguson?" Lance asked. His faded cranberry cambric shirt had sweat stains at the neck while his large black hat protected him from the heat of the midday sun.

"I'm fine, Mr. Gallagher," she whispered, although a tear tracked down her cheek.

He paused and shifted from foot to foot. "If you don't mind me saying, you don't look it. What did that man say to upset you? If you don't want him to visit again, that can be arranged."

She sputtered out a laugh at his suggestion and shook his head. "He's an upstanding member of the community and my neighbor. Nothing can be done to him." Her voice broke. "Whereas I...I'm looked upon with suspicion and mistrust." She closed her eyes and wrapped her arms around her middle.

"That's pure nonsense," he said as he rested his arms on the floorboards to the porch and peered up at her. "That man has an agenda, and you can't allow him to make you believe he's looking out for anyone but himself."

She took a deep breath and met Lance's worried gaze. "How do you know that? You've never seen him before today."

He raised his eyebrows. "I've seen him here before, usually from a rooftop. Plus, I've met enough men to know the type."

She swiped at her cheeks. "Zachariah will be furious," she whispered.

"As he should be. No man has the right to come onto your ranch and threaten you." Lance glowered down the drive as though still able to shoot the long-departed Sterling Hayden.

She shook her head. "No, Zachariah will be more upset that I gave up the ruse of the docile woman." She half smiled when Lance snorted. "Zachariah thought I'd have more success if the townsfolk believed he was in charge."

"Then they're all half-wits not to have suspected the type of woman you are." He studied her a moment. "Or you've spent your time hiding on your ranch so few would discover the truth." He nodded when she flushed as though he'd discerned the truth with little difficulty.

"How did you know it?" she whispered.

"I knew within the first five minutes of meeting you." At her inquisitive stare, he smiled. "When you asked what I'd fix. Women with no interest or understanding in running a ranch would have remained silent or deferred everything to Zachariah. You stood beside him as his equal."

She ran a hand over the fabric of her skirt. "Alan always hated that." At Lance's inquisitive stare, she murmured, "My husband. My late husband. He wanted to be fully in charge even though he had little aptitude for it."

He waited for her to say more, but she remained quiet. "What does your neighbor want?"

She shook her head in resignation. "He claims he wants the land, but I know he wants my water." She met his knowing gaze. "Mr. Hayden was furious when he found out I'd secured majority water rights to the creek coming from the mountain. His land has a creek, but it dries up by August each summer. Too often his cattle wander onto my land."

Lance scratched at his head. "Has he tried to divert the creek?"

She nodded. "I believe he has, although I can't prove anything. A large tree fell into my creek last year, diverting the water toward his lands." She sighed as she rubbed at her forehead. "The creek had run in the direction of his land many years ago, but strong runoffs had diverted it to fully flow on my land. The branch of the creek that fed his land dried up around the time we got the ranch."

"That can happen," Lance said with a shrug. "The tree falling into the creek and the creek drying up."

"Perhaps, except with regard to the tree falling into the creek. It's important to know that no trees were in that area for miles. Just little shrubs," she said as her cheeks flushed with anger. "When I removed the tree, placed strategically where it would divert water into his dried-up creek bed, he tried to claim I was 'disturbing nature's tendency to distribute her bounty in a fair manner.'" She shuddered. "I've never seen him so irate when I informed him that he had no right to prevent me from removing the obstruction."

Lance looked at her as he stood to his full height. "Be careful, Mrs. Ferguson. You and your boys. When a man becomes irrational, you don't know what he's capable of." He tipped his hat and moved away to continue his work.

L ance rode into town a few days later after having received a message from Reverend Brown to visit that day at 2 p.m. Lance resented the summons and did not like leaving the work that needed to be completed. However, he knew the work would always be there, and he was smart enough to heed Jack Hollis's warning to not ignore the reverend's summons. Lance listened to the sound of a distant *boom* as dynamite sounded in one of the mines. Carts and wagons filled the streets of Rattlesnake Ridge, and men loitered outside the popular saloons. Few women walked down the street, and this was still mainly a man's town. He wondered at the fact Miss Eleanor was not more highly sought after by the bachelors of Rattlesnake Ridge and then focused on maneuvering Amaretto through the traffic. A little ways down Main Street, he could see a flow of customers entering and exiting the General Store, and the café seemed particularly busy for this time of day.

He turned his horse in the direction of the church and approached the preacher's small house. Located behind the church, it was whitewashed with black shutters beside the windows on either side of the door. A covered porch protected the entrance-way, and Lance scraped his boots on the boot scraper, although there was no mud this time of year in arid Nevada. After taking a deep breath, he took off his hat and knocked on the door.

A broad-shouldered, austere-looking woman with gray hair pulled back into a severe bun answered the door. She looked Lance up and down and then motioned for him to enter. He recognized the silent, severe looking woman as the reverend's wife. He left his hat on a peg by the door and followed her into the immaculate dining room next to the entryway. On the other side of the entryway was a small living area. Closed doors to the rear of the house separated the rest of the living quarters from visitors.

The dining room had two windows, covered in a thin, gauzy curtain to afford privacy but to allow light to enter. An intricate lace tablecloth covered the round table, and Lance fought a grimace at potentially spilling his tea on such a pristine item. The table had been set with a delicate tea service of china. On the walls were two photographs of what he assumed were relatives, and there was a cased cabinet to hold the fine china.

He remained standing as she bustled from the room. After a moment, he turned at the sound of footsteps and smiled as Reverend Brown entered the dining room. "Hello, Reverend," Lance said with a deferential nod of his head. He held out his hand when the reverend extended his.

"Mr. Gallagher, such a pleasure to see you on this fine day." The reverend's brown eyes twinkled at delight at his visit. "Please, sit." He motioned to the table, and Lance sat at one of the places set for tea.

Lance noted three place settings. "Will your wife join us?"

"Aye, she will. She enjoys meeting the new arrivals to town." He beamed at his wife as she entered the room with the pot of tea. "Adeline, I believe you've met Mr. Gallagher."

She nodded at Lance and set the pot of tea on a tile. "Welcome to our home," she said as she sat down. She passed around a plate of raisin bread and then filled up teacups. She noted Lance's grimace and frowned. "Do you not like tea, Mr. Gallagher?"

He flushed and then smiled with embarrassment. "I'm unaccustomed to drinking it on such a warm day."

She smiled and added a dollop of milk to it. "I find the best discussions occur over a cup of tea." She looked at her husband as though daring him to disagree with her.

Reverend Brown chuckled. "I would have said

whiskey, but I'm inclined to agree with her. Although, whiskey can elicit the truth where tea doesn't." He saw his wife's mouth twitch as she fought a smile. "I fear we will always prefer to have tea in the afternoon, due to our roots."

"Do you miss Scotland?" Lance asked.

Reverend Brown shrugged. "It seems we were destined to live in a place of rain for part of our lives and a desert for the other part." He smiled as he sipped a cup of tea and then clasped his wife's hand. "It can be difficult to be separated from family."

Lance nodded and played with the silverware in front of him.

"Come, Mr. Gallagher, tell us where you're from," Adeline Brown asked in a no-nonsense voice.

Lance took a small sip of his tea and looked from the reverend to his wife and then back again. "I suspect the sheriff should hire the two of you as detectives." That earned a chortle from Adeline. "I was most recently in Deadwood. I found I had no desire to remain after the outbreak of smallpox." He shifted in his chair as they watched him intently. "I wandered and ended up here. Thankfully, Mrs. Ferguson's advertisement appeared in the paper here as I was passing through, and I visited her ranch that day. I enjoy my work."

The reverend sat back and crossed his hands over his belly as he studied Lance. "How providential you should drift through town just as her advertisement came out."

Adeline nodded. "It was her fourth."

Lance shifted in his seat again, feeling much like a recalcitrant school child awaiting punishment. "Yes, it was quite fortunate."

The reverend paused and then said, "You seem taken with her boys."

Lance raised his eyebrows and then scratched at his forehead as he attempted to decipher the question that had not been asked. "I enjoy her boys, yes. They are good helpers at the ranch."

Adeline took a sharp intake of breath. "Do you mean to say that Mrs. Ferguson is allowing those boys to aid you?"

Lance nodded and took a bite of bread in hopes of being able to skip answering a question.

"Remarkable," she murmured. "She's swaddled them as tight as newborn babes since her husband died, and I've feared they'd grow up not understanding the meaning of good, honest work."

Lance choked on the dry bread and took a hasty swallow of tea. "Well, Mrs. Brown, they seem to relish whatever task I put before them. Except for mucking out stalls."

The reverend laughed at that. "Oh, how wonderful. And Zachariah? How is he managing?"

Lance looked at them with confusion. "Well. He's a fine foreman." He frowned as he saw them exchange glances. After a moment, he cleared his throat. "Perhaps you could help me with something, Reverend. I remain confused as to the ferocity of your recent sermon and the unease it provoked in Mrs. Ferguson."

Adeline grunted with displeasure. "It is because some in this town are blind to the facts and prefer to listen and promulgate falsities so as to hear their own voices."

Lance stared at her with his mouth agape as he attempted to decipher what she had just said. "Do you mean women like to gossip?"

Adeline gave a swift jerk of her head in assent.

"That's a universal truth. Heck, most men I know like to gossip as much as any woman." Lance stared at the couple, still puzzled.

"Perhaps," the reverend said as he took his wife's hand in his. "However, there is a difference between idle chitchat about someone's dog eating a pie cooling in the windowsill and attempting to ruin a woman's reputation and future."

Lance stiffened. "Who would attempt to harm Mrs. Ferguson?" He glowered at the couple. "And who would be foolish enough to believe the rumors?"

Adeline watched him appreciatively. "Exactly. Only fools. Or those bored with nothing better to do. It's the devil's work to stand around all day and gossip." Her cheeks flushed with her anger.

Lance traced the handle of his fine teacup. "I know this sounds like I am gossiping, but I am trying to understand. It seems as though everyone in the church understood your sermon but me. What is the gossip?" When they remained closemouthed, he sighed. "I fear I can't help dispel ridiculous notions if I don't know what is being said."

"To speak such untruths gives them credence," Adeline said. "Mrs. Ferguson knows what is being said about her in town. If you wish to know, you should speak with her." She looked at Lance with approval. "However, I am most impressed by your show of loyalty today."

She poured him another cup of tea and nodded to her husband. The reverend cleared his throat. "Now, my boy, tell us more about yourself."

Lance soon found himself the subject of a not-so-subtle inquisition where he felt compelled to answer each question. Toward the end of the barrage of questions he said, "I sold my homestead, rather than live on it alone. The solitude of such a place, when I'd had my dreams dashed..." He cleared his throat and looked at the crumbs on his plate. "It was more than I could bear." He looked up as Mrs. Brown made a commiserative noise. "I never want to hurt like that again," he whispered.

"To live is to hurt," the reverend said. "You must hope that you have someone by your side who helps ease the ache."

Lance looked up sharply to meet his gaze and then nodded in understanding. He rose to leave the table and stared at Mrs. Brown with reluctant admiration. "If I didn't know better, I'd swear you slipped whiskey into my tea. You have a powerful way of urging those around you to speak the truth."

Adeline beamed at him. "It's why my husband and I make such a formidable team."

Lance shook the pastor's hand and then walked to the front door with Mrs. Brown where he smiled his thanks. When he stood outside, he took a deep breath and shook his head as he thought about all he had discussed. He put his hat on and approached

Amaretto, eager to return to the ranch and to escape the inquisitive couple.

Eleanor opened the rickety gate to her kitchen garden and sighed. Somehow a rabbit had found its way in and had decimated an entire row of sprouting cabbage. She looked around and saw a gaping hole in the wire fence. "How could that have happened?" she muttered to herself.

Securing the gate behind her, she walked to the barn. "Why I bothered to shut the gate is beyond me," she muttered to herself. "Any creature smaller than a bear could squeeze through that gash."

Lance looked up from working with one of the horses. "Is someone hurt?" He was instantly alert and appeared ready to race to aid whoever needed help.

"My garden," she said with a glower. "The fence is in need of repair."

He smiled and relaxed. "Let me finish with Cream, and I'll fix it." He gave a click to the horse and urged it to trot at his bidding. When she continued to watch him rather than return to her garden, he said, "I'm making sure a few of your horses are tame enough for the boys to ride. Many of them seem a bit too…spirited."

She fought a glower and met his curious gaze. "Alan liked horses that were a challenge. He said they would prove to live longer."

Lance chuckled. "An odd theory." He gave another click, and Cream slowed down. "Let me rub her down, and I'll meet you at the garden." He walked into the barn with Cream docilely following him.

She watched in wonderment, murmuring, "I've never seen Cream do that." After a moment, she grabbed a bucket, filled it with water, and lugged it to the garden. Once there, she tugged her hat firmly over her head and knelt at the start of one of her rows of carrots. "I'm glad something interrupted the rabbit before it got here," she said as she removed weeds. Soon, she had worked her way down one row and then up another.

With a sigh, she rose and reached for a shovel. She saw Lance approaching with wire, pliers, and another bucket of water. "You shouldn't carry heavy buckets from the barn," he admonished.

She swiped at her forehead and rested her hands on her hips, marring her brown work dress with streaks of mud and soil. "I saw the bucket and thought to fill it up there. I generally use the hand pump by the back door of the kitchen." She smiled as he looked disgruntled and as though he wanted to argue further with her. "If I don't keep the garden watered, it will die. And I like to keep the root cellar stocked as much as possible for winter." She took a deep breath as she rested.

"Why don't you have your boys do the chore?" Lance asked as he moved to the gaping hole at the side of the fence.

"They will help, but they turn watering the garden into a competition and waste water as they rush around." She shook her head.

He paused in studying the fence to look at her. "A few drops of water here and there aren't going to lead to ruin."

She shrugged. "I live in fear the wells will run dry. It's happened to others, and I want my boys to respect that we live in a beautiful, but harsh place. Water is one of our most precious assets."

He smiled. "Remarkable." He focused on the fence and didn't comment further as she worked on hilling the potatoes. He looked up and glared as he saw her work. "You shouldn't be doing such hard work."

She paused, panting as she caught her breath.

"Mr. Gallagher, I'm certain you've met many women who work harder than I. If I want this ranch to succeed, and I do, then everyone must work hard and do their part. Myself included. A little digging in the garden has never hurt me."

He watched her with concern as he fingered the wires in the fence. "Miss Eleanor," he called out. He flushed and hastily said, "Mrs. Ferguson, will you please look at this?"

She set aside her shovel and swiped at her forehead again with the back of her arm as she moved around rows of vegetables. When she stood on the opposite side of the fence with him, she met his worried gaze. He continued to touch the wire, and she shook her head in confusion. "What is the matter?"

He reached forward and gripped her hand, tugging her fingers free of her work glove. "Feel." She flushed as he touched her bare hand and then focused on the wire. "I don't understand. It's smooth."

"Exactly," he said with a satisfied nod. "Too smooth." He handed her glove back to her. "Someone cut this fence. Wanted your garden to be ruined."

She looked around as though she could see the

person who wished her garden destroyed. "Who would do such a thing?"

He shrugged as he tugged on his work gloves. "I couldn't say, Miss ... Mrs. Ferguson. I would recommend you try to determine who would wish you harm." He cleared his throat. "And I'd consider getting a dog. It'd alert you to strangers on your land."

She half smiled. "The boys have always wanted a dog."

"They have good instincts," he said with a smile. "This won't be hard to patch up. But you want to make sure it doesn't keep occurring. A little lost cabbage never hurt anyone." He fought a smile as she glared at him indignantly.

"Are you implying my cabbage crop is inferior and won't be missed?"

He laughed. "No, ma'am. I'm saying not all of us like cabbage. I won't mind a meal without pickled cabbage. And I'm sure your boys or Zachariah feel the same."

She fought a smile. "Well, Mrs. Wagner has always insisted that cabbage is healthy for us."

"And it is. Just not every day," he said. "Oh, and Miss...Mrs. Ferguson? I'll water your garden every evening from now on."

She looked at him as he bent to work, attaching new wire to the severed wire. "Please call me Miss Eleanor if you prefer," she whispered. "And there's no need for you to do the watering."

He looked up to meet her shy gaze. "Oh, there's every need." He nodded to her once and focused on his task again as she returned to hilling potatoes. They worked in companionable silence until she moved inside to avoid the heat of the day.

CHAPTER 5

In early August, Lance watched as the two boys raced away from the ranch house and heard them chattering about swimming in the creek. He swiped at his forehead and envisioned taking time away from his mountain of chores to join them. Instead, he returned to the barn for more nails before making his way to the chicken coop. When he entered the wired-off area, he tried to *coo* to the chickens, but they scattered, clucking their displeasure at his arrival.

He chuckled and began to whistle as he stood on a ladder to work on the roof. Soon, he was hammering loose shingles in place before he worked on replacing missing boards. He peered into the coop through a gaping hole and shook his head at the flimsy shelter the chickens had had in the winter. Soon, he had shored up the chicken coop, and he escaped their domain with only one peck on his behind.

Dripping with sweat after working on the chicken coop, he decided he had earned a break after weeks of hard work. Gathering a worn towel, fresh clothes, and a bar of soap, he ambled in the direction the boys had scampered in. No breeze stirred, and the only sound was that of the grasshoppers clacking as they flitted away from him as he strode down the path. Each step of his boots caused small puffs of dust to rise from the parched earth. Looking to the cloudless, bright blue sky, he sighed as there was little hope for rain today. Or, he feared, any day in the near future.

As he approached the creek, he smiled upon hearing the boys' laughter and voices. Suddenly, there was a scream.

"Peter!" Simon's panicked voice screeched.

Lance took off at a run, his towel and clothes forgotten as he dashed in the direction of Simon's voice. He skidded to a halt when he reached the edge of the creek that bowed out to form a small pondlike area and frowned. "Simon, what?" he gasped as he saw the boy in the shallow area of the pond.

"Peter hit his head and fell in," Simon sobbed as he stared at the water, his hands reaching down, searching for his brother. "He sank."

Lance kicked off his boots and strode into the water, his hands searching for an arm or a leg. He dove under the water, blindly feeling for anything that felt like part of a body. When his lungs burned, he returned to the surface, took two gasping breaths and dove under again. This time, his hands collided with what felt like a leg, and he yanked. He grunted and pulled harder as he dragged Peter to the surface.

"Peter!" Simon screamed.

"Back up," Lance gasped as he pushed the boy to the edge of the pond. He pounded on Peter's back and then on his chest. "Come on, Peter," he pleaded as he pushed on his chest again. Water spurt out of Peter's mouth, and Lance pushed him on his side as Peter coughed when he sucked in air.

"Peter!" Simon yelled as he threw himself at his older brother.

Lance grabbed Simon, holding him to his chest so that he wouldn't knock out what little air Peter had managed to gasp into his lungs. "Shh, Simon. He'll be all right." When Simon had calmed he asked, "Will you go down the trail a little ways and fetch my towel?"

Simon ran away and returned a minute later with his ratty towel. Lance wrapped it around Peter's head, the back of which oozed a steady stream of blood. When the towel was secure, Lance stood and picked Peter up into his arms. "Simon, as we head back to the house, will you please find my spare clothes and the bar of soap I dropped?"

He followed the younger brother at a more moderate pace, murmuring his approval as Simon hollered after he found each article of clothing and then the bar of soap. Soon, Simon raced past him toward the house, bellowing about Peter's calamity.

"Your brother will have your mother in a state by the time you arrive," Lance murmured to Peter.

"Head hurts," Peter whispered as he rested against Lance's shoulder.

"I know, boy. But you'll recover," he murmured. "You'll be just fine." As he rounded the side of the barn, he looked up at a screech reminiscent of Simon's to see Eleanor racing down the porch steps toward them. Her arms were outstretched, and she nearly barreled into them. Lance took a step to the side to prevent her from hitting them and knocking Peter out of his arms.

"Steady, Miss Eleanor," he murmured. "Your boy will be fine. He has a head wound and a headache, but he'll be fine." He waited as Eleanor ran shaking hands over her boy before she stepped back and nodded.

"Yes, please, follow me." She marched back to the ranch house and held the door open for him, pointing him upstairs. "His room is to the right at the top," she said as she followed him up.

When Lance entered the small room with a single bed and a miniscule table beside it and a chest of drawers, he stood to one side. "Perhaps you want to place a towel or blanket on the bed so as not to mar that fine quilt," he murmured.

Eleanor's arms were filled with sheets and towels, and she dropped them on the corner of the bed before pulling a sheet over the bed and then placing a towel on the pillow. "Please, set him down." When Peter rested on his bed, she ran a hand with loving tenderness over his forehead. With a deep sigh, she stiffened her shoulders and pulled the towel off. Fresh blood poured from the head wound, and she hastily covered it again. "I fear this may need stitches," she whispered.

"I can go for the doc in town, Miss Eleanor," Lance said. At her decisive nod, he strode from the room and raced down the stairs. He paused when he saw Simon hiding near the foot of the stairs. "Peter's fine, Simon. I have to get the doctor so he can stitch his head wound closed."

"*She*," Simon blurted out. "Our doc's a lady."

Lance smiled. "Seems your town is more unconventional than I realized." He ruffled Simon's hair. "Hold down the fort while I'm gone, all right?" He saw Simon's chest puff out at the request, and he smiled at the boy. "I'll be back as soon as possible."

Lance ran to the barn, saddled Amaretto, and pushed him into a full gallop as he raced for town. He remembered the doctor's office being next to the bank, and he was thankful he wouldn't have to ride through town in his pursuit of the doctor. When he arrived, he tied Amaretto to the hitching post and barreled into the small office. He whipped off his hat and came to an abrupt halt as the petite woman behind the desk rose to stare at him in confusion.

"I beg your pardon, Doc," he said as he nodded in deference to her status in town. He looked down at his splotchy clothes covered in blood, mud, and dust. "Are you the doc?"

She waved away his apology. "Yes, I'm Dr. Wright. What's happened?"

"Peter Ferguson fell and hit his head. He's at the ranch, but Miss...Mrs. Ferguson fears he'll need stitches." He paused as she pushed past him. "You'll come?"

"Of course I will," she said as she pulled on a light coat, a bonnet to cover her dark curly hair, and gloves. "I'm Gracie Wright, by the way."

Lance nodded.

Her medicine bag sat on a table by the door, and he grabbed it for her as she reached for it. "Did you come in a wagon?"

Lance paled. "No, I rode to town as fast as I could."

She sighed. "Come." She led him through an examining room, out a back door, and into the area behind her office. A small lean-to barn stood with a horse sleeping inside. "It will take a few minutes for me to saddle my horse."

He shook his head and handed her bag to her. "Let me," he said as he moved into the stall. He spoke with her horse in a gentle tone and soon had the horse saddled. He helped the doctor up and handed her the bag. "My horse is out front."

"I'll meet you there," she said as she urged her horse into motion.

Soon, they rode to Broken Pine Ranch, although not at as quick a pace as Lance had raced into town. She watched him clench and unclench his jaw.

"Eleanor is smart. She knows what to do to prepare for my arrival. Peter will be fine," she soothed.

Lance nodded. "I worry about infection."

Gracie sighed. "It's the greatest concern when there is a wound, but I hope you know I'll do all I can to ensure he remains healthy." She patted her horse and urged him a little faster.

They passed fallow fields, baked brown under the unrelenting summer sun. In the distance, a few scattered ranch houses that backed into the hillsides could be seen, although few cattle were visible. They turned down the drive to the Broken Pine Ranch, and Lance sighed with relief.

After he helped the doctor from her horse, he brought her horse into the barn. He curried him and ensured he had plenty of water and a pail full of oats. He then did the same for Amaretto, adding words of praise for his stalwart horse.

With his chores completed, he returned to the house, easing the door open. Simon sat on the second step of the stairs, tears coursing down his cheeks as Peter screamed upstairs. "Come, it can't be as bad as you imagine," Lance whispered as he sat next to Simon and slung an arm over the boy's shoulders.

He leaned against Lance and cried into his side.

"It should have been me," he whispered. "I chickened out and wouldn't do that jump, so Peter did."

Lance gave a grunt of displeasure. "Then you showed more sense than your brother. He should never have been up on those rocks, and now he's paying for his folly. But he'll be all right. Anyone who can bellyache the way he is will be fine."

Simon giggled but remained in Lance's embrace. "Mama always told us never to go on those rocks. She never likes us to go swimming alone. She never wants us to do anything alone."

Lance smiled at his grumbling. "You're her boys. She wants to protect you."

Simon's blue eyes peered up at him. "Did your mama keep you tethered like that?"

"No, Simon, but I was working a farm by the time I was your age. Free time meant spending the day at church, listening to the reverend, rather than tilling a field."

The boy frowned at him. "That doesn't sound like much fun."

Lance laughed. "It was the life I knew. We all had to work hard so there was food on the table and so we wouldn't lose our farm."

Simon sighed, his shoulders stooping. "Mama has us do chores, and I'm no good at them."

"Take pride in all your work, Simon. No matter how little or unimportant you believe it to be. You never know what it will teach you."

Simon picked up Lance's hand and stared at the scratches, scars, and calluses. "I want hands like yours."

Lance's hold on Simon tightened a moment as he was filled with a deep emotion for the boy. "I want yours to be not quite so rough. It will mean your life hasn't been as tough as mine."

Simon settled into his side, and they listened to the quiet murmurs and soft footsteps upstairs. Peter's crying had abated, and a sniffle was heard now and then. "He'll be all right, Mr. Lance?" Simon whispered.

Lance kissed his head. "I hope so. I know your mother and the doc will do everything they can to ensure Peter recovers."

When footsteps sounded on the stairs, Lance looked over his shoulder and then urged Simon to stand. Dr. Wright walked downstairs, holding her medicine bag. "Doc?" he asked.

She smiled at Lance and then at Simon who clung to the ranch hand. "Peter should be fine. He didn't like having stitches placed, but his wound does not appear serious as he is awake and lucid. Do you want to go see your brother, Simon?" The minute she asked those words, Simon raced up the stairs to see his big brother.

"He's a wonderful boy," Gracie Wright said.

"They both are," Lance said with a nod. "Thank you for coming to help Peter." He flushed after he spoke as he realized he had no position on the ranch to thank the doctor for her service.

She watched him closely and nodded. "It was my pleasure." She stood on the final step of the stairs and was closer to eye level with him. "Ensure Eleanor doesn't fret. Her boys need to act like boys, not coddled and wrapped in cotton." She waited until Lance nodded before she moved to the kitchen, calling out for Mrs. Wagner.

Lance remained at the foot of the stairs, uncertain if he should go upstairs. After arguing with himself for a few minutes, he walked upstairs and poked his head into Peter's small room. It felt overcrowded with Simon and Eleanor inside. "Miss Eleanor," he murmured as he saw her clinging to Peter's hand as her free hand continued to flit over his shoulder and arm.

"Mr. Gallagher. Thank you for all you've done today."

He shrugged. "It's nothing, ma'am." He focused on Peter. "How are you feeling?"

Peter opened his pain-dulled eyes and looked at Lance. "Awful."

Lance fought a smile as he lowered to his knees so he was at eye level with the boy. "That's what happens when you hit your head and need stitches."

"I don't ever want stitches again," he said in a small voice.

Lance gave a grunt of agreement. "Yes, they are no fun, but thankfully a good doc is in town to help care for you when you need her." Lance looked at Eleanor. "Did she leave something for infection?"

Eleanor nodded and pointed to a small container. "An ointment that I should put on his wound twice daily. And we'll give him willow bark tea for his pain."

Lance squeezed Peter's shoulder. "You're in good hands, Peter. Follow your mother's instructions, and you'll be playing with your brother again soon." He squeezed his shoulder again and rose. "Miss." He nodded to her and slipped from the room.

He returned to the barn, organizing the tack room and mucking out stalls as he waited for the doctor to request her horse. Leaning against the wall, he fought panic at all that could have happened to Peter. Lance battled against his desire to be anything more than a hired ranch hand. For that was all he ever could be.

That evening, Eleanor sat beside Peter as he slept. She had dragged her comfortable chair in from her bedroom, and now his room felt even tinier. However, she was determined to keep vigil overnight in case he needed something. Her knitting needles clacked softly as she worked on a pair of socks. She frowned as she focused on forming the curve at the ankle, thankful for any distraction from her racing thoughts. When she had to pull out the yarn due to miscounting for the third time, she sighed and set down her needles.

Peter rested comfortably after drinking a large mug of willow bark tea and showed no sign of fever. Simon snored softly from the room across the hall, and Mrs. Wagner was in her room downstairs near the kitchen. Eleanor hated her desire to have a man in the house to feel more secure. She'd fought the inclination to have Zachariah live in the large ranch house after a family of skunks had infested the foreman's cabin the previous year. Smiling, Eleanor remembered Simon's joy at watching the skunk family roll down a hill as they played in the middle of the night, illuminated only by the bright moon. Her smile faded as she recalled his dismay when he learned they had been relocated. Eleanor huffed. "Relocated," she muttered. "To a shallow grave." Neither she nor Zachariah had had the heart to inform her youngest son that they had exterminated the intruders.

Eleanor rested her head against the top of her chair and sighed with pleasure as a gentle breeze ruffled the curtains covering the open window. An owl hooted, and a wolf howled in the distance. "Stay away from my cattle," she muttered.

She opened her eyes and focused on Peter, rather than the roiling visions her imagination conjured when she closed her eyes. His peaceful expression. His face subtly changing from a boy's to a man's. Her throat thickened with tears she refused to shed as she saw glimpses of Alan. His strong chin, small button nose, and thin lips. Unlike Alan, her Peter was quick with a smile and a joke and was willing to work.

Her gaze moved to the window, and she pulled back the curtain, glancing toward the bunkhouse. A sliver of moon cast light upon the yard, and she failed to see any movement at the bunkhouse. Shaking her head, she marveled at all Lance had done for her and her boys that day. With Zachariah away, she did not like to consider what would have happened had she been alone on the ranch with one of her boys injured. She refused to consider her boys alone and helpless at the swimming hole.

She jumped as Mrs. Wagner bustled into the room on near silent feet. "I didn't hear you," she whispered.

"No, you were woolgathering about that new ranch hand," Mrs. Wagner said with a severe stare. Her blue eyes shone with concern, although her customary disapproval of Mr. Gallagher was absent.

"I don't know what we would have done had he not been here," Eleanor whispered.

"We would have done what we've always done. Coped," Mrs. Wagner said in her no-nonsense way. "It was nice to see he had more sense than your husband ever had." She nodded as Eleanor flushed and did not contradict her.

Mrs. Wagner looked into the water pitcher to ensure it was full. "And he had the sense not to be upset that our doctor is a woman."

Eleanor held her hand up and cut off Mrs. Wagner. "Unlike Alan."

Mrs. Wagner gave a curt nod of her head. "Just so. There comes a time when all that matters is that the person doing the required task is competent. I've never seen a person less squeamish about the unsavory aspects of life than Dr. Wright."

Eleanor shuddered. "I can't imagine being a doctor, but I'm very thankful she chose to live here."

"And her husband had the sense to marry her," Mrs. Wagner said. She motioned for Eleanor to stand up and pushed her out of the way as she sat with a relieved sigh in the comfortable chair. "Go get some fresh air, Eleanor. You need a break."

Eleanor flushed and pulled her shawl more tightly around her although the night was far from cool. "Your matchmaking won't work, Mrs. Wagner. He's not outside." She blushed beet red at her frank words.

"Go, girl," she said with an imperious nod of her head to the door. "Let an old woman rest as she keeps vigil."

Eleanor kissed Mrs. Wagner on the forehead and spun to depart. "I'll be back in a few minutes."

"Of course. We all need a respite from duty, dear," Mrs. Wagner said with a smile as she watched the woman she considered a daughter smooth her unbraided hair and ease from the room.

Lance sat on the rocking chair on the bunkhouse porch, watching as Eleanor emerged from the ranch house to lean against a post to stare out at the darkened landscape. The faint light from the ranch house illuminated her soft curves and her hair cascaded down her back, freed from its customary tight bun. He gripped his hands, closing his eyes as he imagined the silky soft feel of her hair slipping through his fingers. "She's your boss," he muttered to himself as he forced his muscle to relax.

"What did you say?" her gentle voice called out.

He fought an instinctive urge to reach for a pistol that no longer sat at his hip when startled, and forced a smile as she approached him with a lantern in hand. "I said, 'What a mess.'" He rose and motioned for her to sit beside him in the spare rocking chair.

She nodded and sat, setting the lantern between them. "It is. I can't imagine what the boys were doing playing in the creek with no supervision." She shuddered. "If you hadn't decided to join them…"

He made a soothing sound. "But I did. Peter was injured, but at least they don't have to regret the loss of a brother." After a moment he asked, "Who is sitting with Peter?"

"Mrs. Wagner. She wanted me to have a break, but she understands that I don't want to leave Peter alone tonight." She covered her mouth as she yawned. "It's a nice respite to be out of the house for a few minutes." She grimaced, unable to fight a guilty expression from flashing across her face.

"There's no reason to feel guilty that you need a few moments away. That doesn't make you a bad mother, Miss Eleanor."

She looked at him with luminous blue eyes and nodded. "A part of me knows that. Another part of me feels like, no matter what I do, I will never be an adequate mother."

"Adequate?" he asked, raising his eyebrows in surprise. "Is that all you think you are?" He shook his head and smiled. "You are exemplary in your love and devotion to your boys, Miss Eleanor. Don't ever doubt yourself."

She shook her head. "I should have searched for them when I noticed they weren't playing near the house..." Her voice broke.

He paused, and he spoke with hesitancy as he chose his words with care. "They need to run and play and work without you or Zachariah or anyone always around. They need to test their limits and learn what they can and cannot do."

She made a derisive noise and glared at him, her blue eyes lit with fire. "How can you say such a thing when I almost lost Peter today?"

He pinched at the bridge of his nose. "The worst thing you can do is swaddle them up and keep them close like they were still babes. Give them wings, Miss Eleanor." He jerked his hand back as he reached to grip hers.

"You don't know what you're asking," she whispered. "You don't know what it is to lose someone you...care about."

He rose and leaned against the post holding up the roof covering the porch. "Don't I?" he whispered. He looked out in the direction of the barn, but his gaze was distant. "I have a better idea than you might imagine." He turned to face her. "I know what it is to lose someone I love, Miss Eleanor. Not someone I merely cared for." His eyes glowed with pain and passion.

She gasped, her hand rising to clasp her shawl more tightly around her shoulders. "Who?"

"My wife," he whispered. "My daughter." He cleared his voice as it broke as he mentioned them. "Died from the typhus while I was away, trying to sell our cattle for a decent profit four years ago." He shook his head as he looked at her. "Nothing was worth the loss of them."

"Oh, Mr. Gallagher," she whispered as a tear tracked down her cheek. "I'm so sorry."

He gave a sharp jerk of his head in acknowledgment of her sympathy. "The point is, everyone has had their share of sorrows, Miss Eleanor. We all carry hidden wounds we'd rather not lay bare."

She gave a bitter laugh. "Yes, but my sorrows are the source of town gossip and ridicule." She rubbed at her temple and hunched her shoulders as though to protect herself. She looked at him with confusion as he knelt in front of her and took her hands in his.

"Do you know that, those few days I spent in Rattlesnake Ridge, no one spoke of you in anything but the most complimentary terms." He shrugged. "Men die in card games. It's an all-too-frequent outcome when you gamble your common sense along with your money."

She shook her head and ducked her chin. "You wouldn't hear the gossip," she whispered, her voice laden with anger.

"I don't understand. The men in the saloon mentioned your husband and quickly moved on to another topic." He squeezed her hand in encouragement.

Eleanor's blue eyes shone with anger as she met his inquisitive gaze. "Women won't gossip with men, but they truly run the town. They determine who is accepted. Who is deemed worthy. And if you aren't, then you will be shunned."

He shook his head in confusion. "Who would dare shun a woman who has the gumption and intelligence to run a successful ranch?"

She rose, breaking her contact with him. "Thank you for your conversation, Mr. Gallagher. I will always be indebted to you for the service you did my boys today."

He clamped his jaw tight in frustration. "I care for them, Eleanor. You know that."

Her startled gaze met his at his use of only her first name. "I do. And I'm ever so grateful you do." She grabbed the lantern and brushed past him, scurrying back to the ranch house.

He watched her hasty retreat, replaying their conversation over and over in his head, but unable to decipher what she had wanted to tell him. "Why can't she speak plainly?" he muttered as he listened to the door slam shut at the ranch house.

He sat again in the rocking chair and allowed the

soothing motion to ease his tension. He fought, and lost, the battle of recalling his wife. A petite woman with shiny black hair, his wife, Amy, had taken great pride in their homestead in the Colorado Territory, in his plans to expand their small holding. When their daughter, Laura, a spitting image of his wife, had been born, he had fallen to his knees in thanksgiving because he knew he would never again know such immense joy as seeing his wife holding their child in her arms. He took a deep breath as he'd never known a greater sorrow than when he'd had to bury them four years later. He bowed his head and whispered, "I'm sorry," to the wind.

Thinking about his wife and daughter brought back the longing for family he attempted to suppress. For home. For a sense of belonging. He feared he was becoming too attached to Peter and Simon and would need to move on soon. "For they aren't mine," he whispered. "And they never will be."

The following morning, Lance sat on his front porch, sipping a cup of coffee as he watched the sky change color. Streaks of pink chased away the darkness until it was replaced by a gentle glow.

He sighed and was about to heave himself up for another day of work when he saw Simon racing from the house in his direction. He settled again in his chair, waiting for the boy to arrive.

"Simon," he said with a welcoming smile. "I never expected you to be awake this early."

Simon climbed onto the other rocking chair, the one his mother had occupied the previous night, and rubbed at his eyes. "I'm not generally. But Mama and Mrs. Wagner woke me."

Lance saw the boy curl into himself with his worry, and Lance reached a hand out. "Peter will be fine. He hit his head, but you heard him screaming at the top of his lungs when the doc was here to patch him up. He'll recover and toss you into a horse trough soon enough." He frowned as Simon failed to smile, and a tear leaked onto Simon's cheek. "Simon?"

Simon vaulted from his chair and clambered onto Lance's lap. "I know I'm too big," he muttered as he curled into the man's embrace.

"No, boy," Lance whispered as he held Simon and rubbed at his back. "Peter will be fine."

"This time," Simone whispered. "What about next time? What happens if you're not around? Or Zachariah? Or Mama?" His voice hitched with his panic. "I couldn't have saved him. He would have di-i-ied." He burrowed his head against Lance's chest as he cried.

"Shh," Lance whispered as he held the sobbing boy. "You and Peter did nothing wrong. You played in your swimming hole, and there was an accident." He looked up as he saw Eleanor race onto the ranch house porch, her gaze frantic. He raised his arm, and she seemed to calm when she saw him cradling her son. After a moment, she returned inside.

When Simon quieted, Lance kept his hold on the boy. "Here's the problem as I see it, Simon. Your mother will now be even more worried about you than before. She will want you and Peter to do even less than you did." He saw Simon nod. "Is that what you want? To be in the kitchen or the garden with your mother?"

Simon shrugged and rubbed at his nose. "I like the kitchen. Mrs. Wagner gives me more treats now that Mama spoke with her."

Lance chuckled. "I can see it has its merits."

Sniffling, Simon said, "But I like being in the barn with you. Learning how to work with horses. Running around with Peter." Simon frowned as he looked at the older man. "Why can't I do it all?"

Lance nodded. "Exactly, Simon. You should do it

all." He gave him a pat and urged him to rise. "Come, let's wash up and join the others for breakfast."

They walked to the pump in front of the barn and washed their hands and faces. When they arrived in the kitchen, no scent of bacon or eggs greeted them. Lance tilted his head, and he heard the women speaking upstairs. "Come, Simon. It's our turn to help your mother and Mrs. Wagner. I suspect they've both slept very little." He urged the boy to the kitchen, where he pulled out two frying pans.

He stoked the wood in the kitchen stove, adding wood so their food would cook, and then searched for a bowl. When he looked around for eggs, he sighed. "Simon, will you collect the eggs?" He handed the boy a basket and nodded to the back door. He smiled as Simon raced away. While the boy was gone, Lance brewed coffee, sliced up thick slabs of bread, and readied the bacon for frying.

Soon, Simon dashed into the kitchen, and Lance winced as he looked into the basket. However, none of the eggs had cracked in Simon's sprint from the chicken coop. "Well done, Simon," Lance said as he taught Simon how to crack the eggs and then scramble them. Soon, he flipped the bacon and had the eggs cooking in the other pan. When the bacon was close to done, he fried the bread to make toast.

"How'd you learn to cook? I thought only women knew how to cook," Simon asked as he watched with curiosity and fascination as he knelt on a chair to better see the frying pans on top of the stove.

"I would've starved many times if I hadn't learned how to cook basic things," Lance said with a smile and a wink to his young friend. He took a long sip of coffee and sighed with pleasure. "It's a luxury for me to live in a place where I eat such good food every day." He watched Simon with curiosity as he made a face.

"Except for the pickled cabbage," Simon grumbled, and Lance laughed.

"Shh," Lance whispered as he leaned over in Simon's direction. "I agree with you, but you would never want to offend such a good cook."

A few moments later, Mrs. Wagner bustled into the kitchen area. "What are you doing, working at my stove?" she demanded, her hands on her ample hips. The darkness under her eyes was a testament to her fatigue.

"Simon and I feared you and Mrs. Ferguson were tired after caring for Peter all night," Lance said.

"We made breakfast!" Simon said as he thrust his hands up in a celebratory way.

Mrs. Wagner smiled and nodded. "Good. I had

feared we would make do with slabs of bread with butter this morning."

Lance winked at his collaborator. "That's what we feared too."

Mrs. Wagner sat with a deep sigh at the table.

"Simon, sit with Mrs. Wagner," Lance said, filling three plates with food and setting two on the table for them. "I'll bring Miss Eleanor a plate and see if Peter is awake and hungry."

He pushed the frying pans to a cooler part of the stove where the food would stay warm, but not overcook, and then left the kitchen. He ascended the stairs and paused as he heard a lilting singing from Peter's room. He closed his eyes as he battled memories of his wife singing in a similar manner to his daughter. After a moment, he took a deep breath and made a loud noise with his boot heels. "Miss Eleanor?" he asked in a loud whisper.

He poked his head into Peter's room to find the boy sleeping. Eleanor sat in a large chair at the foot of his bed, her knitting needles and a ball of yarn forgotten at her feet. Her reddish-brown hair tangled around her shoulders, and her blue eyes had a glassy look to them. He recognized an exhausted woman and knelt by her chair, setting the plate of food and cup of coffee next to him on the floor.

"Miss Eleanor," he said in a soft voice. "Please eat and drink some coffee. And then go to bed. I'll sit with Peter while you rest. Simon is fine and with Mrs. Wagner." He saw her delayed attempt to formulate an argument. "Any work, I might have, can wait. Nothing is more important than you or the boys."

She nodded and then leaned forward, her head resting against his chest. "I'm so tired. So tired of worrying on my own. Of having no one to lean on."

His breath came out in a stutter, and he ran a hand over her shoulder. His fingers became entangled in her hair, and he held her in a sort of embrace for a few moments. "You're strong, Miss Eleanor."

She leaned away and shook her head. "Forgive me. That was...uncalled for." She flushed and refused to meet his gaze.

"I disagree. We all have limits, Eleanor, and there's no shame in admitting that." He waited for her to nod and frowned when she continued to avoid his gaze. When she stood, he rose and stepped away. "Your food."

"I'll make another plate downstairs," she murmured, pushing past him.

Lance watched her leave, his hands fisted as though forcing himself not to reach for her as she scurried away from him and out of the room. He sat with a sigh in the chair she vacated and stared at the slumbering Peter. After a moment, he heard Eleanor's soft voice downstairs as she spoke with Simon and Mrs. Wagner. He berated himself for separating himself from the shared meal but then focused on the fact he had given her a respite from her caregiving duties.

A few minutes later, he picked up the plate of food he'd prepared for Eleanor and dug into it. He grunted with pleasure to realize his food was good, although not nearly as savory as that prepared by Mrs. Wagner. When finished, he set the plate on the bureau and stretched his legs out again. He held the cup of coffee between his palms and settled in to watch Peter.

After he had drained his cup of coffee and set the cup on the floor, he crossed his arms over his belly, closed his eyes, and began to whistle. He whistled tunes he learned from the army, from cattle drives, and from his wife. The ones from his wife were the sweetest and brought a slight ache to his chest. When he finished one song, he opened his eyes to find Peter peering at him.

"Hello, Peter," Lance murmured in a soft voice. "How are you feeling?"

"I'd be doing better if you stopped that horrible

noise," he complained, holding a hand to his bandage. "My head hurts enough as it is."

Lance chuckled. "I'll see if it's time for more willow bark tea." He rose and rested his hand on Peter's shoulder. "Rest and recover, Peter. You'll be fine."

Peter looked at Lance and gave a subtle nod, grimacing as that movement made his pain worse. "Thank you for saving me yesterday."

Lance smiled. "I'd do it again without a moment's hesitation." He smiled at the boy and headed out to find Mrs. Wagner and some tea for his young charge.

That evening, Eleanor walked across the barnyard to the paddock where Lance stood facing away from her. She saw him stiffen at the sound of her footsteps, and, although she faltered in her approach, she joined him at the rail. A halfmoon lit the barnyard and paddock, and horses snuffled as they dozed in the covered structure. She sighed as she lifted her face to the stars and closed her eyes with pleasure at the slight breeze that cooled her face. "Heaven," she whispered.

"Yes," he agreed.

She opened her eyes to find him watching her rather than the stars or the surrounding scenery. She flushed at the implication of what he had just said.

"I cannot thank you enough, Mr. Gallagher," she said in a low voice. "I … I can't bear to think about what …" Her voice broke as she was unable to finish that sentence.

"It does not bear contemplation," he said in a gruff tone. "Your boy is well and will recover. He'll be more cautious for a while."

She shivered. "I hope he is cautious from now on."

Lance chuckled. "He's a growing boy. He's meant to know no fear." He looked at her. "Don't steal that innocence from him."

"What are you afraid of?" she whispered and then ducked her head as though embarrassed at the question. "I beg your pardon. I have no right to ask you something so personal."

He shrugged. "You have every right to ask, just as I have every right not to answer." He waited as he saw disappointment glint her eyes. After a long moment, he whispered, "Losing everything again. I don't know if I'd survive it again."

She froze, and then her eyes filled. "I beg your pardon. I'm not generally so insensitive."

Lance leaned away from the paddock as though stretching out his arms and then stood straight again. "I don't expect you to remember my sorrows, Miss Eleanor. They are burdensome enough for me." He paused and then whispered, "What do you fear?"

She took a stuttering breath. "Trusting a man who doesn't merit my regard."

He looked at her for so long she flushed. "I fear your husband was a disappointment, Miss Eleanor."

She scoffed and shook her head. "I know Zachariah has already told you about how we came to be here at this ranch. That Alan won it at a game of cards." She looked at the outline of the mountains visible under the moon's light. "I give thanks every day for that stroke of luck. Otherwise, I fear I'd be toiling away as a seamstress or in a mill."

"With land, there is security." He watched her nod. "At least you are secure in your ownership of your ranch. You don't have to worry about a bank coming after you." He frowned as she shifted in discomfort. "Miss Eleanor?"

She looked at him and gripped the paddock railing more firmly. "We do have a loan."

He leaned toward her as though he hadn't heard

her correctly. "I beg your pardon?" he asked. "How? Why?"

She firmed her jaw and looked straight ahead. "Did you imagine that, from the time he won the ranch to the time he died, he never gambled again?" She made a derisive noise. "He gambled frequently. When he was low. When he felt invincible. When…" She closed her eyes as though in defeat. "He never needed a reason. He had losses that had to be covered. And I refused to sell any of the land. He would have whittled us down to twenty acres." She shuddered. "I give thanks every day that he never bartered the ranch."

Lance covered her hand with his. "I never imagined what that would be like." He squeezed her hand. "I'm sorry."

She shrugged. "How were you to know?" She took a deep breath as she attempted to allow the calming evening air to soothe her. "No one was ever to know. We were the happy couple, with the perfect children, living on a ranch we never should have been able to afford. Our life was supposed to be perfect."

He gave a small *tsk*ing sound at the bitterness in her voice. "But it was far from perfect, wasn't it?"

"Yes," she admitted. "From the moment we

married, it was a struggle. It should have been wonderful. I never thought to see him, walking down the lane, thin and battered, but alive, after the war. I thought I'd mourn his memory forever. Instead ..." She rubbed at her forehead with her free hand. "I shouldn't burden you with this."

"It's not a burden, Eleanor," he whispered. He met her gaze as he said her name. "I hope you will consider me your friend as well as your ranch hand."

She smiled shyly at him. "I do," she said in a soft voice. "I've held these truths so tight that it's hard to let them out. I was taught to never let others see the truth of what I was feeling. To never let my disappointment show."

Lance watched her with tenderness. "You are a survivor. And you have thrived. You should take great pride in that."

She sniffled. "Yes, but I live in fear that my boys will have an overwhelming desire for risk. For gambling. As their father did." She shuddered at the thought. "And that fear keeps me awake at night."

He stroked a hand over her forearm. "All you can do is teach them well. And trust that they will follow in the example that you set for them." He paused as they listened to the evening noises of coyotes crying in the distance and an owl hooting. "What do they say about you in town?" He gripped her arm as she attempted to jerk away. "I mean no disrespect. I merely want to understand so I know what nonsense it is and can refute it."

"How do you know it is nonsense?" she asked.

"Because I see how it hurts you. Because the reverend wouldn't have spent two sermons on it if it were true." When she bit her lip and remained undecided, he whispered, "Trust me."

She closed her eyes, and a tear slipped down her cheek. "They whisper that Simon isn't my husband's. That he is Zachariah's."

When Lance was quiet for a prolonged time, she opened her eyes to see him staring at her with abject confusion. "They would doubt your honor?" His eyes flashed with rage.

"You can see why." She sniffled. "Simon does resemble Zachariah in certain ways. He has black hair and blue eyes."

Lance waited for her to say more and then held up his palms. "That's it? He has black hair and blue eyes? You have blue eyes. Why should it matter if he has black hair or blond hair? That shouldn't spark gossip."

"They say Alan intentionally provoked the man

to shoot him because he was ashamed of my perfidy."

"Your deceit?" Lance took a step toward her and touched her softly on her shoulder. "Don't they know you at all? How can people who've known you for years doubt you?"

She looked at him with wonder. "How can you not doubt?"

He smiled at her and traced a finger over her cheek. "I've seen you. You're loyal and honorable and kind. You worked hard to shield your husband's weaknesses from those in town. You never would have cheated on him." His eyes glinted with his anger. "I understand now why Mrs. Brown was so irate."

Eleanor froze. "You asked her?"

He nodded. "Yes. I wanted to understand. I felt like the only person in town who didn't comprehend the warning behind the reverend's sermons." He smiled at Eleanor as his finger continued to trace a pattern over her cheek. "You have a strong ally in Mrs. Brown. She refused to speak aloud the gossip because she said to speak it would give it truth. She is a formidable woman."

Eleanor huffed out a laugh and nodded. For a moment she leaned into his touch, and then she forced herself to back up a step. "Well, now you know. Now you understand why I have so few visitors." She stepped away from the paddock railing. "I should return to Peter," she said as she looked down as though embarrassed.

"Good night, Miss Eleanor," he whispered. "I hope Peter continues to recover well."

"Thank you, Lance," she murmured before she spun on her heel and returned to the ranch house.

The following day, Lance knocked on Peter's door and smiled as the young boy looked at him with relief. "Happy it's someone other than your mother and Mrs. Wagner?" he asked with a chuckle. He entered and sat on the chair at the foot of the bed.

Peter had a fresh bandage wrapped around his head, he wore a clean set of pajamas, and a sheet covered him as he lay on his bed. A book was by his side, although it remained unopened.

Lance frowned. "Why aren't you reading?"

Peter grimaced. "The words are jumbled and blurry. It makes my head hurt worse." He sighed. "Mama reads to me when she has time, and Simon tells me stories. But I think he prefers to be outside, working with you."

Lance nodded and set his small package at the foot of the bed. "He does. He's determined to learn how to hammer as quickly as I do. So far, he's nearly busted three fingers." He shook his head as he looked at Simon's older brother. "He will forever try to keep up."

"No," Peter said. "He'll surpass us. That is how Simon is." He smiled with brotherly pride.

"I'd think you'd find your younger brother more annoying than you do." Lance leaned forward and rested his forearms on his knees as he studied Peter.

Peter shrugged. "I'll always be older and wiser, but I'll never be as brave as Simon."

Lance frowned. "Then why didn't Simon go on those rocks? He said he refused, and you taunted him. That that's why you fell."

Peter paled, and his eyes rounded.

Lance said, "Ah, Simon fibbed." When Peter nodded, Lance rose. "Simon?" he called out and waited as he heard the clatter of his young feet running downstairs and then clambering up the stairs. "I have a question for you," he said to the youngest brother when Simon stood in front of him. Lance shut the door to afford them privacy.

"Yes, Mr. Lance?" he asked.

Lance placed his hands on his hips and furrowed his brows. "Why did you lie to me?"

Simon paled, and his gaze shot to his brother for an instant before he looked back at the man waiting for an answer. "I… I didn't want Mama to know the truth. She's already worried about me," Simon whispered. He ducked his head as though in shame.

Lance sat down, and he was at the youngest boy's eye level. "Don't lie. You almost always get caught. Either because the person you were with was truthful or because you can't remember your lies." He sighed and pinched the bridge of his nose. "Besides, your life is better if you are truthful."

"Why?" Simon asked in a small voice. "Mama is always mad at me when she realizes I've acted wild again."

"That is a question you must ask your mother. She has fears to face, and you can help her confront them," Lance said in a gentle voice. "However, you should try to always tell the truth." He smiled at Simon. "I don't want to be a hypocrite as we all tell little fibs here and there."

Lance sobered as he looked at the young boy. "However, your fib about what occurred at the swimming hole was a big one. Will you tell me what really happened?" He paused and then murmured, "And then you must tell your mama. It's not fair she's angry with Peter."

Simon hung his head, and his shoulders stooped. "I challenged Peter to a race to our swimming hole. An' then after we played a while in the water, I said I was gonna jump off the rocks." His voice became animated as he told his story. "I love climbing as high as I can, and I wanted to make a big splash." He held his arms out wide.

"What happened?" Lance asked as Simon became serious.

"Peter insisted he had to go first because he was older." Simon looked at his brother as guilt marred his expression. "I was mad because it was my idea."

"Simon?" Lance asked.

"I called him a scared monkey and that even Isabelle could climb the rocks faster than he was." Simon sniffled. "He tried to climb faster and tripped." Simon fought tears as he looked at his brother. "I'm sorry, Peter."

"You're my baby brother, Simon. I'd rather have this headache than you," Peter said.

Simon sniffled. "No one should." He leaned against Lance's knee and accepted Lance's hug. "I'll tell Mama. Promise."

"Good," Lance said as he patted him on his back. "But, before you do, I wondered if you'd play a game of checkers with me?"

"Checkers?" Simon asked, lighting up and bouncing on his toes. "Yes!"

Lance laughed and opened the box he'd brought with him, setting it on the end of Peter's bed. Simon stood, while Lance sat on his chair. Simon insisted on being red, as Peter was always red, and he wanted to be red for once. "Fine," Lance said.

He looked up at Peter and saw him smiling with his eyes closed as he and Simon set up the board. "Prepare to lose," Lance teased the young boy.

Simon continued to chatter throughout the four subsequent games, talking about the horses, the stream, the chores he would do because Peter was ill. Through it all, he matched each of Lance's moves, and they were tied two games each.

"One more, Mr. Lance?" Simon asked as he bounced around by the side of Peter's bed.

Lance chuckled and agreed. "I wish I could bottle up your energy," he murmured. As he and Simon set up the board, he looked at the young man. "Simon, a word of advice, man to man." He saw Simon pause in putting down his checkers as he focused on him. "Always try to speak properly.

Only swear when there's nothing else you can say."

"All the boys talk rough," Simon said with a frown.

Lance nodded. "I know. They talked rough when I was a boy, too, and it's all right to talk with your friends like that. But with adults, or someone of authority, always speak properly. You'll earn their respect faster."

Simon bit his lip. "Is that why you never swear or say things like *ain't*?"

Lance laughed. "Yes, although I do in my head sometimes."

Simon bit his lip as his eyes danced with mischief. "Do you cuss in your head?"

Lance shook his head. "Yes, Simon, but I try not to let the bad words out."

Simon nodded. "I think I understand." He sighed and focused on the board. "I bet I can beat you."

"I bet you can, too." He reached across and ruffled Simon's hair before focusing on their checkers match.

Two days later, Gracie Wright rode down the lane and smiled as Lance emerged from the barn to greet her. "How's my patient?" she asked as she handed him her reins. She swung down from the horse and then reached for her medicine bag and a small bundle that squirmed.

Lance stared at the bundle but smiled his welcome. "Better. He's getting fidgety and wants out of bed."

Gracie laughed, wearing a serviceable navy dress and a broad hat to protect her face from the bright sun. "That's a sign that he's recovering well. I assume Eleanor has kept him bedridden?"

Lance grinned at the doctor as she turned purposefully toward the house. "Yes, although I think she realizes she will soon fail in that endeavor."

Gracie laughed again and smiled her thanks as Lance grabbed her medicine bag. "Well, hopefully I will find him much improved, and he can roam the ranch again." She giggled as the bag she held squirmed.

"Might I inquire what you have in that bag?" Lance asked.

She beamed at him. "Eleanor mentioned the boys needed a puppy. Our dog just had a litter a few months ago, and we'd be delighted for the boys to have him." She opened the flap, and a furry head popped out with floppy ears. He had a white head except for a black patch covering one eye.

Lance grinned at her. "It'll be fun to watch the boys' reaction. And to see them argue about naming him."

She smiled. "Yes." She cuddled the puppy. "Sometimes the best medicine has nothing to do with medicine."

He watched her with even more respect and followed her inside and up the stairs. Before she went into the room, she exchanged the puppy for her medicine bag. "Keep the surprise," she whispered.

He nodded and sat on the floor in the hallway, holding the puppy as it turned in circles to settle on his lap. He ran a soothing hand over its back as it quivered with fright. He sighed with relief when it lay down and gave a gentle snore as though it were falling asleep.

He listened to Gracie talking with Peter, exclaiming what a great patient he had been, and soothing Eleanor's fears about infection. "What a wonderful doctor," Lance murmured. He relaxed further when he heard Peter giggle, and Eleanor laugh, as Gracie told a story about a miner who had come in after his partner had accidentally pickaxed him in the backside. "As you can imagine, he won't sit down for some time!" Gracie said with a laugh.

After she gave instructions for Peter, where he was advised he could move around again, but not to resume all of his wild antics, she informed him, "I have a surprise for you and your brother."

Lance rose and ducked into a room off the hall as the doctor summoned Simon. Lance heard Simon's excited footsteps and high-pitched voice, murmuring to the puppy to keep it quiet, afraid that any barking would ruin the doctor's surprise. He glanced around the room he'd entered and froze, belatedly realizing he was in Eleanor's room. On her bureau, he studied a picture of her with a severe-looking man who stood stiffly beside her. He frowned as he noted little warmth or caring in either expression. "I wonder if that was her husband?" he murmured as he studied the austere gentleman with narrow shoulders. He jerked as the door was opened.

"There you are," Eleanor said, and she flushed as she caught him staring at the items on her bureau. A silver brush and hand mirror set. A small box where she kept little treasures. And the only picture of her and Alan. "Gracie's ready to give the boys her surprise." Her expression softened as she focused on the adorable puppy in his arms. "Oh, aren't you precious?" she breathed as she traced a hand over the puppy's head.

Lance stepped toward her, wishing she were referring to him. He froze and backed away a step. "I'll follow you in," he rasped as he cleared his throat. "I beg your pardon for invading your private space, but I did not want to ruin this for Simon."

"I understand. Follow me," she said as she turned to reenter Peter's crowded room. "I found him!" she called out.

Lance took a deep breath and walked in after Eleanor. For a moment, there was complete silence in the room as the boys gaped at him. Then Simon gave a *whoop* and hopped around while Peter jumped to his knees and opened his arms.

"Give him to me!" Peter said.

Lance shook his head. "This adorable puppy comes from Doc Gracie and her family. From what the doc told me, she wants it to be for both of you boys, not just one of you. Is that correct, Doc?" Lance looked to Gracie to find her fighting a fit of the giggles.

"Yes," she said. "This puppy is for both of you."

Lance nodded and motioned for Simon to join

Peter on the bed. When the brothers were sitting side by side, he set the puppy between them. At first, the little creature gripped Lance's shirtfront with its claws, but after a few moments it huddled between the brothers.

Simon reached forward and patted its back. "So soft," he whispered as he continued to pat the white dog with black splotches.

Peter stroked its ear and giggled when the puppy licked his hand. "What should we call him?" he asked his brother.

"Spot!" Simon said as he traced one of the black areas on the puppy.

Peter shrugged. "Maybe, but that seems obvious." He smiled as the puppy squirmed between the two of them. "What do you think, Mr. Lance?"

"He's your puppy, boys. You should name him," Lance said as he knelt by the side of the bed, flipping the puppy's inside-out ear back in place.

"But, Mr. Lance, you should help us," Simon said as he tried to ease the puppy closer to him. He stilled his not-so-stealthy movements when Lance gave him a warning stare. "Sorry," he whispered to Peter.

Lance looked to Eleanor who nodded her encouragement at him helping her boys name their puppy. He pointed at the puppy's eye. "I thought Patch would be a good name."

"Patch," Peter said and then looked at his brother. "What do you think?"

Simon raised his hand up in triumph. "Patch!"

Lance smiled at their enthusiasm. "Now, having a puppy isn't all fun and games. You have to ensure he's not just laying around, eating all the time. And you must train him to only go to the bathroom outside, like we do." He winked at the boys as they giggled.

"Where will he sleep, Mama?" Peter looked to his mother. "In the barn?"

Lance frowned at the question and looked at Eleanor in confusion as she flushed. "The barn?"

"Alan disapproved of animals being inside the house. However, I believe young Patch will be most welcome here." She smiled at her sons. "He should have a small bed that travels from Simon's room to Peter's room, depending on where he sleeps each night."

"It should be his choice," Simon said.

"Simon," Eleanor said with a warning in her voice. "You know my position on food upstairs. You will not entice the puppy to your room with food. I believe what would be fair is that Patch spend every other night with each of you."

Simon nodded, although he looked as though he were plotting some way to spend more time with his puppy. "All right, Mama." He smiled at his brother. "We have a dog!" He squirmed and hopped from the bed. "Get dressed and come play outside. We can teach him how to fetch!"

He tried to grab Patch, but Lance beat him to it. He winked at Simon. "I'll carry him downstairs for you. It might take him a few days to learn how to navigate the stairs." He watched as Simon raced down the stairs, calling out that he would find the perfect stick for their puppy.

"I'll tend your horse, Doc," Lance murmured, as he followed Simon out.

After Peter dressed and followed Simon and Lance downstairs, Gracie and Eleanor sat on the front porch to watch the boys play with their puppy. Simon tried to have the puppy fetch a huge stick, and Eleanor laughed as the puppy toppled over in the attempt to drag it. Soon, the boys tossed a small stick and then played tug of war with Patch, until Patch let go, and they could toss the stick again.

"Thank you so much for coming to check on Peter again today." Eleanor looked at her son, laughing and playing with his brother, and fought tears. "I can't tell you what it means to see him well."

Gracie nodded. "I'm delighted to see how well he has recovered. But, that's the young. They recover so quickly." She smiled at Eleanor. "I will return in about a week to remove his stitches. He'll be none pleased with me that day."

Eleanor nodded. "I'll remind him that you brought him Patch." She sobered as she looked at Gracie. "Are you sure your family doesn't mind giving us such a wonderful dog?"

Gracie flushed and looked down. "I must admit something, Eleanor. Patch is the runt of the litter, and I feared we wouldn't find a home for him. We already have too many dogs as it is."

"My boys will never think of him as a runt," Eleanor said. "Are you busy in town?"

"As busy as I want to be," she said as she smiled at Mrs. Wagner who brought out a pitcher of water and two glasses. After murmuring her thanks, she said, "There is rarely a dull day in Rattlesnake Ridge."

"I should think you'd dream of a dull day now and again," Eleanor murmured. "You were so competent when you arrived here. Cleaning Peter's wound and then sewing him up. You never faltered in your task, even when he screamed and carried on." She fought tears at the memory. "I don't know how you have the fortitude to do it."

"We all do what we must. And this is what I was meant to do, Eleanor. I love my work." She sighed with pleasure. "I'm fortunate I found a man who does not resent my desire to continue to work even though we are married."

"A rare man indeed," Eleanor murmured as she sipped at her water. Her gaze wandered to Lance, and she fought a blush as Gracie caught her.

"My hope is that you are as fortunate as I am." They sat in companionable silence for a few more minutes until Gracie rose. "I fear I have another call to make, and I'd like to return home before it is too late."

Eleanor walked with her to where her horse dozed in the shade of the barn. "Thank you, Gracie."

Gracie nodded and then smiled at Lance as he helped tie her medicine bag to her horse and then gave her a hand up onto her horse. "I can do it alone, but it's always nice to have help. Notify me of any changes!" She waved to the boys as she rode away.

"A remarkable woman," Lance said as he watched Gracie a moment.

"Yes," Eleanor murmured as she fought a stab of envy.

He shot a quick glance at her. "It appears this area has more than its fair share of them." He nodded deferentially and entered the barn, leaving her gaping after him.

CHAPTER 6

By early September, Zachariah had returned to the ranch and had begun to make arrangements for the fall roundup that would occur in October. The cattle were fat and content in the upper pasture, and he would join his men at the end of the month to drive them down to the lower fields before driving the cattle to the railroad to be sent to Chicago. Zachariah ran a soothing hand over his horse's muzzle as it limped. "Shh, Rogue," he murmured.

"What's the matter?" Lance asked as he saw Zachariah leading his horse into the barn.

"He threw a shoe, and we have no blacksmith," Zachariah said. "The farrier hasn't been here since mid-July, and I fear he's too busy in town to make a journey out here to see us."

Lance nodded. "I saw a shed near the far side of the paddock with smithing items. I used to shoe the horses at the ranch I worked on. I'm not a farrier, but I know what I'm doing." He saw Zachariah brighten at his words. "Let me see what I need, and I'll fire up the coals." He approached Rogue and lifted up his unshod hoof, examining the hoof. He then lifted up another hoof and studied the horseshoe.

At Lance's nod, Zachariah led his horse into one of the stalls. When Rogue had settled, he followed Lance to the old blacksmithing shop. Zachariah bit back a smile as he saw Lance glowering at the dust-covered, chaotic room. "You didn't think it would be in any different a state than the barn had been in, did you?"

Lance sighed and then chuckled. "There is a little bit of coal, which should be enough for today's needs. But we should get more." He dusted off the anvil and found tongs and different sized hammers. He grinned at Zachariah. "I always loved my time in the forge, although it felt like hell on earth during hot summer days in …" He bit his lip. "In Kentucky."

"Deadwood, South Dakota. Kentucky," Zachariah

said as he ticked off places he knew Lance had lived. "Colorado. Now Nevada." He met the man's startled gaze. "You have moved around quite a bit."

"I figure, if you end up in Nevada, most people have." He found two large buckets and set one on top of a turned-over one. "I need to fill this with water."

"Wait for the boys. It's a chore they'll enjoy." Zachariah stood with his arms over his chest as he watched the ranch hand move around the space. "Anything of interest occur in my absence?"

Lance shot a quick look at this boss and grimaced. "Peter fell into the swimming pond after hitting his head on rocks and almost drowned." He watched as Zachariah paled, and he feared for a moment that the large man would faint. "Thankfully, I had decided to join the boys for a swim, and I was able to pull him out."

Zachariah spun and looked out the door to the ranch house. "How is he? El?" He ran a hand through his raven hair. "I should see them."

Lance gripped his shoulder. "Calm down first. Miss Eleanor has finally relaxed her grip on the boys, and they are running free on the ranch again." He grinned. "With their puppy, Patch."

"Puppy?" Zachariah parroted. He met Lance's grin. "About time those boys had a dog."

"Doc Gracie brought them one of her pups, and he's gnawing his way through the house. I think Miss Eleanor regrets her decision to allow him inside." Lance chuckled. "Last night I thought she would banish him for good when he'd eaten her Sunday-best gloves."

Zachariah grimaced. "Whoops."

"Word to the wise. Leave nothing out that you don't want him to chomp on. He's already mangled a bridle I left lying about." He shrugged. "He's a dog. We shouldn't expect him to act other than he is."

Zachariah sobered. "Peter is well?"

Lance nodded. "Yes, he needed stitches and a few days in bed, but he's fine. And it taught Simon a good lesson, too." He watched as Zachariah frowned. "Simon taunted Peter, and Peter fell. Simon is feeling quite a bit more reticent, although he still runs around like the little wild man he is most days." He ducked his head as he was unable to hide the hint of pride in his voice when talking about the boys.

"They are fortunate you've taken such a shine to them," Zachariah said.

He shrugged. "What did you find in the high country?"

"We were a man short. One of the men left to work for higher wages for Sterling." He clamped his jaw shut. "How that man could entice away one of our workers when he was in a high mountain pasture, is beyond me."

Lance shook his head. "And it's hard to believe Sterling has that much capital in the middle of a depression. Most would make do with the farm hands they have, rather than stealing their neighbors' hired help."

Zachariah nodded. "There's the measure of the man. He's determined to obtain this ranch, and he'll do what he must. His family has always been successful, and I think he doesn't understand adversity well."

"He sure doesn't understand when a person doesn't agree with his plan," Lance muttered. "He and Miss Eleanor had a disagreement while you were away."

"I was afraid of that." He looked at Lance a long moment. "Sterling's aware she's much smarter than he thought, isn't he?" At Lance's amused grin, Zachariah frowned. "Well, it was only a matter of time before they figured out she was the brains behind the whole operation."

Lance continued to work in the blacksmith shop, and Zachariah said, "If you can shoe my horse soon, why don't we go for a ride and look over another part of the ranch this afternoon? The evenings are still long."

Lance nodded. "I'd like that." He smiled as he heard the boys racing around as they searched for him. "I'll work with my little helpers while I shoe your horse, and then we can head out."

"Mr. Lance! Mr. Lance!" Simon called out as he hopped up and down. "Whatcha doin' in here?" He poked around the dirty blacksmithing shop and giggled when a puff of dust enveloped him after he pushed on the bellows. Coughing, he peered out at Lance.

"You are incorrigible," Lance said with a smile. "I'm doing a little farrier work for Zachariah. His horse needs a new shoe."

Simon's blue eyes lit up. "Can we help?" He pointed to Peter and himself and puffed out his chest.

Lance nodded. He pointed to the large, empty bucket standing near the anvil. "Yes, it would be a great help to me if you could fill that bucket with water."

Peter groaned and tapped Simon on the arm.

"You're always getting us into more chores." He grumbled as he found a small pail and ran away to the hand pump by the barn. Simon raced after him, calling out that he'd cheated and that he'd beat him back.

After five visits to the pump, the large bucket was filled. Simon stood on an overturned crate while Peter was tall enough to watch everything without a stool. They watched with wonder as Lance used the bellows to heat the coals. "Now, you must promise to obey me while you are in the blacksmithing shop," Lance said in a serious voice. He waited until both boys promised. "You could easily be harmed for life if you don't."

They paled and promised again.

"The coals are very hot and would hurt terribly if you were burned. However, I need them hot so I can mold the steel." He pulled out a piece of steel and set it in the hot coals. He left it in there for a few minutes as he pulled out the tongs he'd use and found a small hammer. "Never touch anything with your bare hands that's been in the fire. Not unless I tell you it's all right."

The boys nodded.

When he pulled out the steel, gleaming red and yellow at the tip, the boys oohed and aahed. When he began to hammer at it, Simon covered his ears and glared at Lance for the noise he was making. Peter laughed at his brother but refrained from calling him a baby.

Lance repeated the process numerous times until he'd formed the piece of iron into the shape of a horseshoe. "There," he said with a satisfied smile as he swiped at his brow and then doused the horseshoe in the bucket of water. Steam rose and made a satisfying hiss as the warm metal hit the water. "I looked at Rogue's hooves when Zachariah brought him to his stall, and I think this will fit him. If not, I'll have to adjust it. Let's hope Rogue only needs one new shoe. If he needs all four, well, that will make for a busy day." He winked at the boys and led them to the barn.

"Rogue's one of my favorites!" Simon said as he ran circles around them.

"He's a beautiful horse. But he's not happy right now because he lost a shoe. I don't want you going into his stall," Lance admonished. He smiled when Simon nodded his agreement. As they walked to the barn, he saw Eleanor sitting on the front porch with Patch on her lap. He waved at her as he walked with her boys.

"Mind Mr. Lance!" she called out to her sons.

"They are, Miss Eleanor," he said with a deferential nod.

"We're gonna see Rogue get a new shoe!" Simon said as he dashed toward her to pat Patch and then raced again to Lance and Peter.

Lance shared a smile with Eleanor before focusing on the boys. "Remember how I taught you to greet a horse," he said as he walked with them into the barn. Soon, Simon and Peter stood behind him as Rogue's hoof was balanced over his bended knee. He trimmed away pieces of the overgrown hoof and then hammered in the shoe. Lance lowered Rogue's hoof and led him to the paddock to watch him walk. When Lance saw Rogue limp ever-so-slightly, he dug around in a bag he'd found in the catch-all room in the barn until he found the tool he looked for.

Soon, he stood behind Rogue again, filing away his hoof. After three attempts, he nodded. "Yes, you'll feel much better," Lance said as he scratched behind Rogue's ear.

"You made Rogue better," Simon said with glee.

"I want to learn how to do that," Peter said. "I can't imagine a better job. When the farrier comes every month, he never lets us watch and will throw things at us if he catches us near him."

Lance frowned at Peter. "I don't remember him visiting since I arrived."

"He hasn't come since July," Peter said. "You were in town that day."

"Mama thinks he finally pickled up and died," Simon said as he played on the paddock fence. "The other farrier is good friends with Mr. Hayden, and Mama didn't want to ask him for help."

"Simon," Peter scolded while Lance fought laughter.

Lance nodded. "Well, it's one more thing I should do. The horses will all need to be reshod soon. It's already been too long for most of them." He rubbed at his forehead and winked at the boys. "I'll need plenty of help from my assistants as I make horse-shoes." He watched when they smiled with glee as they were included in his ongoing work on the ranch.

Lance saddled Amaretto and smiled as his horse gave an appreciative snort. "I know, boy. It's been too long since you've had a chance to run." He gripped the bridle and led him out of the barn before mounting him with ease. He nodded to

Zachariah and followed him down the lane and then headed over a small path into the grassland. Although Amaretto shifted underneath him as though he wanted to burst into a gallop, he continued to trot behind Zachariah riding a freshly shod Rogue. When they reached a rise, Zachariah stopped, and Lance pulled up beside him.

"This is one of my favorite views," Zachariah said. A gentle breeze blew and white billowy clouds filled the bright blue sky. The golden grass swayed in the breeze, and a hawk swooped overhead. In front of them, rolling hills led to the ranch with more hills in the distance. Majestic mountains loomed to their left, a speck of snow at the highest peak all that remained from last winter's fierce storms.

"I can see why," Lance said. He closed his eyes and took a deep breath of the fresh air. "It smells like it might rain."

Zachariah laughed and shook his head. "Now you'll claim you can predict the weather, too."

Lance chuckled. "No, but the day has that feel." He looked up at the brilliant sky. "Although it doesn't look like it will." He shifted in his saddle and looked at his boss. "What aren't you saying about the cattle in the upper pasture?"

He shook his head and patted Rogue's neck. "Not

much gets past you, does it?" Zachariah looked up toward the mountains as though envisioning the summer rangeland. "The wolves are much more active than I'd like. We lost a good dozen cattle this summer."

Lance frowned. "What's your normal loss?"

"Less than half that number." He took off his hat and swiped at his forehead and then tapped his hat against his leg before putting it back on again. "We killed one pack earlier in the spring, but another just took its place."

"And you know it'll happen again if you do the same," Lance said. Zachariah jerked his head in agreement. "You can't make it your mission to kill every wolf in those mountains."

"I know. But times are hard enough right now without worrying about an excess loss due to wolves." He shifted and looked at Lance. "Cattle prices were low last year, and, although they've recovered a little bit, I worry it won't be enough."

"To cover the loan?" Lance asked. He saw Zachariah's shock and nodded. "Miss Eleanor told me about it, although she didn't tell me when the loan was due."

Zachariah sighed. "She's been paying off a piece at a time for a few years. The last payment's due in

November. If we have a good sale this year, then she'll have no difficulty making the payment."

Lance nodded as Zachariah left unsaid his concern. "Well, at least the Great Railroad Strike has come to an end." He saw Zachariah stare at him in confusion. "Railroad workers shut down railroads in Maryland, Pennsylvania, and New York, wreaking havoc. They even closed the railroad for a while in Chicago." He saw Zachariah shudder at that news as their cattle were shipped to Chicago for sale. "But it ended a few days ago."

"What were they hoping to gain?" Zachariah asked.

"A better wage," Lance said as he soothed Amaretto who shifted forward and back as he tired of standing in one place. "Their wages had dropped to nearly half of what they were before the Panic of '73."

"Is that why you weren't upset with only receiving room and board?" Zachariah asked him.

"A job has been increasingly hard to come by. And living on a ranch was always my dream. When I saw Mrs. Ferguson's advertisement, it seemed too good to be true." He paused before murmuring, "Imagine my surprise to realize it wasn't."

Zachariah stared at him a long moment. "Have things progressed between you and Eleanor?"

Lance gaped at him, and he shook his head vehemently. "Of course not! She's a respectable woman."

"Yes, although she is a woman and widowed. I always thought it a shame she believed she would never marry again." Zachariah smiled in a self-deprecating way. "She's smart, stubborn, and loyal. What more could a man want?"

"Nothing," Lance breathed and then flushed as he met Zachariah's knowing stare. "I refuse to compromise her. She deserves—"

Zachariah interrupted him, turning Rogue around so they faced each other. "She deserves a man who respects her intelligence, admires her tenacity, and adores her boys." His blue eyes flashed. "I had hoped you were that man."

Lance glared at his boss. "Are you telling me that you went to the high country so that Eleanor and I would have time alone? So that we could...form an attachment?" He bit out the last words as though they were a curse.

Zachariah's self-satisfied smile provoked a growl of rage from Lance. "Of course." He shifted so he wasn't in range of Lance's right hook. "I wasn't lying when I said I was needed up there. But I also hoped she would come to see you as more than a ranch hand. That she'd see you as a man."

Lance shook his head in disgust. "Darned match-maker. You and Mrs. Wagner probably concocted your plan together."

Zachariah burst out laughing. "If Mrs. Wagner is in favor of you, then you are doing something right." He sobered. "For too long, Eleanor has believed that any relationship with a man was a burden. That she could never have a satisfying relationship with a man." He looked at Lance. "Imagine what her marriage must have been like." He nodded as Lance glowered. "She held the family together, with little support from Alan."

"Why would she believe I'd be any different?" Lance whispered.

"Exactly. You had to prove you were. If I were there, running interference the entire time, she wouldn't have seen it." After a few minutes where Lance stared at the ranch house in the distance, Zachariah murmured, "I hope I wasn't wrong in my estimation of you."

Lance shook his head. "No, but that doesn't mean it's not complicated."

Zachariah laughed. "If it's not complicated, then it's boring and it ain't life." He spun his horse around. "Come on, let's run them for a bit." He urged Rogue into a gallop, and Lance held on as Amaretto eagerly followed.

Eleanor walked to the barn to find Zachariah and Lance. She wanted to ensure they would be at supper. She paused at the barn door when she heard their deep voices. She stiffened as she heard Zachariah murmur, "When do you think you'll tell her?"

Lance muttered, "I don't know how to tell her. Perhaps she doesn't need to know."

"Fool," Zachariah said with a sigh.

Eleanor barged into the barn and glared at Zachariah and then Lance. She stood with hands clamped in fists, her cheeks flushed and eyes flashing with anger. "How dare you attempt to conceal what is occurring on the ranch from me?"

Lance shook his head, but Zachariah approached Eleanor. "El, what are you doing here? We never considered hiding anything from you."

"That's what it sounded like to me," she snapped. She mimicked Lance's voice. *"I don't know how to tell her. Perhaps she doesn't need to know."*

Lance paled. "Eleanor," he whispered.

"Don't," she snapped. "I was taken in once by a handsome face and sweet words. I won't fall for them again." She stood as tall as possible and firmed her quivering jaw. "I want you to leave by sunrise."

"El, you can't mean that!" Zachariah protested. "He's the best worker we've ever had. Besides …" He broke off and swallowed a curse as Lance made a warning sound in his throat.

"Besides what?" she asked as she looked from one man to the other. When they remained silent, she nodded. "You claim you're not keeping something from me, but you're lying." She glared at Zachariah as she fought tears. "You promised you'd never lie."

Zachariah approached her, gazing deeply into her eyes. "Not everything has to do with the ranch." He stormed out of the barn, leaving her alone with Lance.

She stood there, clasping and unclasping her hands together as Lance stood with his back to her. She opened and closed her mouth a few times, unable to find any words to speak now that they were alone.

"Did you mean it?" he rasped. "Do you want me to leave tomorrow?"

She sniffled. "Are you concealing something from me?"

He looked over his shoulder at her, his gaze guarded as he looked at her standing with poise and challenge as she awaited his answer. "Yes."

She flinched as though he had struck her. "Then, yes, I would like you to leave. I have had enough deception for one life."

He flushed with anger and turned to fully face her. "I have never deceived you." He frowned as a tear coursed down her cheek.

"I deceived myself," she whispered before she spun and raced from the barn. She tumbled to the ground when she ran into Simon, hovering near the barn's door and eavesdropping.

"Mama!" Simon protested as she plastered into him.

"This is why you shouldn't listen in on conversations," she rasped as she fought a sob. She pushed herself upright and continued her flight to the ranch house, racing up the stairs to her room. Slamming the door behind her, she wished for a lock on the door so she could barricade herself inside.

Rather than throw herself onto her bed and cry her eyes out as she desired, she forced herself to sit on her comfortable chair as tears coursed down her cheeks. She rocked herself in place, unable to cease sobbing. When the door creaked open, she covered her face with her palms, unwilling to have her grief on display.

"Ah, there's no need for this," Mrs. Wagner said as she closed the door softly behind her. "You've had your first spat with your man."

Eleanor accepted the handkerchief Mrs. Wagner pressed into her hand and swiped at her sodden cheeks. "No," she hiccupped out around her sobs. "I ordered him to leave. He's hiding something from me."

Mrs. Wagner made a noncommittal noise as she pulled over a small straight-backed chair to sit near her. "And do you know what that is?"

"Zachariah claims it has nothing to do with the ranch." She balled the handkerchief in her hand. "I fear it's the first time since Alan died that Zachariah has lied to me."

"Oh, girl. You've had to depend on logic and reason for too long as you managed this ranch. For once, use your heart rather than your head." Mrs. Wagner clasped her hand and waited for Eleanor to meet her worried gaze. "Why else would a man keep a secret from you?"

Eleanor flushed and ducked her head.

"He has feelings for you. They're as plain as day to anyone who looks." Mrs. Wagner smiled as Eleanor shook her head to dispel such a notion. "Is it that you find the idea offensive or surprising?"

"Wondrous," Eleanor whispered. "I thought I…" She flushed. "Why wouldn't he speak to me of his feelings?"

Mrs. Wagner squeezed her hands. "Simon told me how Lance lost a wife and daughter. For a man like him, that would leave a deep scar." Eleanor nodded at her friend's words. "And you're his boss. It does put a man in an awkward position."

Eleanor shook her head. "Why should that matter?"

"The man lost everything. His family. His homestead. His identity." Mrs. Wagner looked out the window as though seeing Lance at the paddock or bunkhouse. "He's found another home here, with you and your boys. I doubt he'd want to risk losing everything again."

She closed her eyes as two more tears tracked down her cheeks. After a moment, she opened her eyes and met Mrs. Wagner's understanding and compassionate gaze. "What should I do?"

"Find a way to ask him to stay," Mrs. Wagner

said. "For, if he leaves, I fear you and your sons will miss him forever."

"Mr. Lance! Mr. Lance!" Simon yelled as he barreled into the barn after his mother careened away toward the ranch house. "You aren't leaving, are you?" He stood there, his blue eyes wide with shock as he watched the man he was coming to dream of as a father move to his horse and begin to saddle it.

Lance refused to look at him as he focused on the task in front of him. "Yes, Simon, I fear I must. I've overstayed my welcome, and I think my work is done here."

"No!" Simon screamed as he hurled himself at Lance's leg and wrapped his arms around his thigh as though his bodyweight would anchor Lance in place. "Don't leave us too." He pressed his face to Lance's middle, his shoulders heaving as he sobbed.

"Oh, lad," Lance whispered as he dropped to his knees and pulled Simon into his arms. "I'm sorry." He held Simon close as Simon sobbed onto his shoulder. "I wanted to stay, but your mama wants me to leave."

"I could ask her to change her mind," Simon stuttered out. "I'll beg her."

Lance ran a hand over Simon's head and shook his head. "That's not fair to her, son. If she doesn't want me here, I should go."

"But I want you here!" Simon sniffled and stomped his foot. "It's not fair she can force you to leave."

Lance held onto Simon's shoulders, waiting for the boy to meet his gaze. "She's your mother, and she's doing what she thinks is right for her family. For her ranch. No one should question her."

"But you like her," Simon protested. He stared at Lance with confusion. "Don't you?"

Lance closed his eyes but did not release his hold of the boy. "What I feel for your mother is between your mother and me." He opened his eyes and met Simon's disappointed gaze. "I want you to understand something, Simon." He waited as the boy sniffled and nodded. "Leaving here will be one of the hardest things I have ever done. I…" His voice broke, and his eyes shone with unshed tears. "I love you and Peter as though you were my own boys. I hope you'll continue to grow into the fine young men I know you can be and that you'll always be a help to your mama."

Simon threw himself forward and wrapped his small arms around Lance's neck. He continued to whisper, "Don't go," over and over again as he clung to Lance.

After many long moments, Lance eased Simon away and stood. He swiped at the tears on Simon's face and whispered, "I have to. I must honor your mama's wishes." He cleared his throat. "Come, help me with Amaretto. For he is going to miss you, too."

A little of Simon's inherent vivacity seemed to vanish, and his shoulders stooped. "Yes, Mr. Lance. I'll miss Amaretto, too." He moved with Lance to help saddle the horse, petting Amaretto on his velvet nose and talking to him in the soft way Lance had taught him, the entire time hoping his mother would enter the barn and change her mind.

Eleanor walked into the barn, and stood stock-still when she noticed Amaretto missing from his stall. "No," she whispered and trotted to the nearby bunkhouse. She knocked on the door, pushing it open when it remained unanswered after a few minutes. She marched inside and froze. The only evidence that Lance had lived here was the faint scent of coffee.

His mattress was rolled up to match the others. No shirts hung from a doorway drying. No socks were slung over the back of one of the chairs. Everything was pristine and in its place as though awaiting the next occupant. "No," she said again as she raced outside and looked up the long drive. No rider was visible, and she would have fallen to her knees had Zachariah not grabbed her around her middle.

"He left, El," Zachariah whispered.

"I...I waited too long," she murmured as she turned her face into her friend's shoulder. "I was vain."

He shook his head in confusion. "I don't know what you mean."

"I didn't want him to see me splotchy faced with red-rimmed eyes. I waited so I'd look more attractive." She covered her mouth with a hand as she fought a sob. "And I lost him."

Zachariah slung an arm over her shoulder and held her close. "That man would never care what you looked like, El. He wants you, as you are."

"I'm such a fool." She wrapped her arms around herself. "Simon will never forgive me, and Peter's hiding in his room, acting like he's fine. But I know he's just as upset as Simon."

"If you leave early tomorrow morning, you have a chance of finding him in Rattlesnake Ridge. He won't have gotten far tonight. Amaretto is tired after a hard day wandering the range." He smiled at her as she watched him with dawning hope. "You hurt him, El. You have to be prepared to humble yourself."

She took a deep breath as she closed her eyes. "That's the hardest part," she whispered. "For so long, I've had to be strong and dependable and know the answer to myriad questions."

Zachariah nodded. "Alan was my best friend, but I'm not blind to his faults, El. You had to carry the weight of responsibility for too long." He paused as though weighing his words. "You have to be willing to share it, or there's no reason to seek out Lance."

She took a step away from her friend and turned to face him, meeting his worried gaze. Wringing her hands together as she considered his words, she whispered, "I am so afraid of giving up any control. What if I'm wrong again, and he proves unworthy?"

Zachariah sighed. "Again?" He smiled gently at her and traced away the tear that tracked down her cheek. "You're brave, El. Braver than you give yourself credit for. What does your instinct tell you about Lance?"

She closed her eyes and took a deep breath, then another. "He's a good man. He cares for my boys." She paused. "It's so hard to overcome this fear, Zachariah."

He squeezed her arm. "If anyone can, it's you." He smiled at her. "So, I should have horses ready tomorrow at dawn?"

Her expression brightened, and she nodded. "Yes. I must find him and tell him the truth. Even if he doesn't return to the ranch, I must know I did what I could."

Zachariah nodded. "I'll see you at dawn, El."

She watched as he walked toward his small cabin while dusk cloaked the ranch. With a sigh, she returned to the house, doubtful she would sleep much that night as she waited for dawn.

Lance rode onto the rangeland rather than into town. Although he no longer worked for Eleanor, he had no desire to be in town and forced to make conversation as he arranged a room at the boarding house or found a meal at the café. Instead, he set up a bedroll on a soft patch of grass near the creek, settled Amaretto, and pulled out beef jerky to snack on.

He sat on a boulder by the creek as he contemplated the day. It had started so well. Talking with Zachariah. Working the forge and sharing that with the boys. Riding part of the ranch with Zachariah. Closing his eyes, Lance attempted to calm his roiling emotions by breathing deeply of the fresh mossy scent of the creek and the melodious sound of the water tumbling over the rocks. However, nothing calmed his sense of unease and heartache.

Visions of Eleanor, standing in front of him, disappointed and disillusioned, filled his mind. He ran a hand through his thick blond hair and berated himself for not having the courage to speak up. To admit his true feelings for her. The fear that clawed at him every time he thought of settling down. Of losing everything he cared about again.

He grimaced when he thought about his conversation with Simon. He flicked at a piece of grass as he remembered fighting the urge to cling to Simon as strongly as the boy had clung to him. "He's not yours," he whispered to himself. He closed his eyes as the truthful agony rolled through him: he wished Simon were. He wished Peter were, too.

He sat for long hours by the creek as he thought about Eleanor and his time at the ranch. For the first time since he'd buried his wife and daughter four years ago, he had found peace. A place he wanted to call home. A woman he dreamed of building a future with. He rose and wandered to his cold bedroll. Rather than unfurl it and curl up inside, he stood staring at the valley illuminated by the bright full moon.

Unbidden, he remembered the reverend's words. *You must hope that you have someone by your side who helps ease the ache.* He rubbed at his chest as he realized that Eleanor was the first woman he could imagine wanting by his side since he'd lost Amy. Running away would not change that. "I must fight her fears as well as my own," he said as he looked at the stars.

"She told me to stay 'til morning," he muttered to himself. "I'll return and speak with her." He hefted his bedroll and moved to Amaretto who nickered in protest as he was resaddled. Rather than ride Amaretto, Lance led him by the bridle over the uneven terrain toward the ranch. He had no desire to wake the family with his arrival, and he wanted more time to consider what he could say to Eleanor to persuade her to believe him.

When he reached the lane leading to the house, he sniffed the air and shook his head in confusion at the scent of wood smoke. Panic filled him as he realized what it could mean and he leapt onto Amaretto's back and raced in the direction of the ranch house. When he arrived, the ranch house was engulfed in flames. Simon and Peter stood flanked by Mrs. Wagner. She kept a firm grip on their shoulders as the boys screamed out for their mother. Zachariah knelt in front of them coughing and gasping for breath as tears coursed down his ash-covered face, muttering that he'd go back in after a moment.

Lance leaped off Amaretto, yelling, "Eleanor?" He knew instinctively that Eleanor was inside. He ran to the water pump by the barn and doused himself in water and then raced for the house. He ignored Simon and Peter screaming his name.

Just as he entered the house, he heard Mrs. Wagner yell to look in the kitchen. As he entered the house with fire licking at the sides of the doorjamb, he gasped from the heat and smoke and pulled up his bandana to cover his mouth. He said a silent prayer that Eleanor was not upstairs as they were engulfed in flames, and he'd have no way to reach her. Crouching near the floor, he half walked, half crawled to the kitchen area. The kitchen was filled with smoke, and the walls were ablaze. He feared the room would turn into an inferno any moment.

He squinted in an attempt to see anything through the thick haze of smoke. After bumping into a chair, he careened into the table. When he righted himself, he swore softly as he stumbled again, only this time belatedly realizing he'd tripped over one of Eleanor's legs.

"Eleanor," he gasped and coughed. He fell to his knees, fighting dizziness and lightheadedness. A loud crash sounded behind him, and a fiery timber now blocked the hallway he'd just walked down. He placed his head close to the floor in hopes for fresher air, but the entire room was filled with smoke.

"The back door," he muttered as he hefted Eleanor up, her body weightless as her arms flailed to the side and her head bobbed backward. His lungs burned as he took a too-deep smoke-filled breath, and he struggled to his feet. He yanked the bandana from around his neck and wrapped it around his hand, twisting the door handle. Although he'd protected his hand, a soft burn still penetrated his palm. After he managed to kick the door fully open, he stumbled onto the back porch and to the backyard.

After walking as far as physically possible, he laid Eleanor on the ground. Glass crashed, and timbers snapped, and he looked over his shoulder to see the kitchen fully ablaze now that the door was open. "Eleanor, please," he rasped as he traced a hand over her cheek. He ran to the water pump near the root cellar and wet his bandana. When he returned to her, he pressed the cool, damp cloth over her brow, face, and neck, frowning when she remained unconscious.

He turned when he heard the boys scream. The house seemed to give another loud groan, and then it toppled in on itself as the flames consumed it. He grunted and picked Eleanor up, moving to the area in front of the house. The boys sobbed inconsolably in Mrs. Wagner's arms while Zachariah was absent.

"Where's Zachariah?" Lance called out in his raspy, smoke-damaged voice.

"Mama!" Peter screamed as he raced toward Lance.

"No, boys," Lance said as he paused. "Let's get her to the bunkhouse. Peter, fill a bucketful of water and, Simon, turn down a mattress." He met Mrs. Wagner's watery gaze. "I did what I could."

She nodded and walked with him to the bunkhouse. On the way there, he saw Zachariah pumping water into buckets and tossing it over the barn and paddock.

"I'll help you in a minute," Lance said as he walked slowly to the bunkhouse.

Zachariah looked at him and dropped his bucket to the ground as he raced to him. "El," he breathed. "Oh, thank heavens. I couldn't bear to watch the house burn and know..." His eyes gleamed with unshed tears and rage. When Zachariah realized that Lance was on the verge of falling over, he eased Eleanor into his arms. "I'll carry her." He nodded as he saw the reluctant agreement in Lance's gaze. "She'll know all you did."

Lance watched as Zachariah walked to the bunkhouse with Eleanor in his arms. Lance coughed so hard he thought he'd never stop, then collapsed to his knees. Finally, he caught his breath, gasping as he took a deep inhalation. Cool hands traced over his face, and he looked up to see Peter watching him. "I'm fine."

Peter walked to the pump and filled a bucket of water. He held out the ladle for Lance and watched as Lance took a long sip of water before dumping the bucket over his head. "Why'd you do that?"

"I need to rid myself of the feeling that I'm still in

a burning house." He watched as Peter nodded. "Get Simon. We have work to do."

Peter raced to the bunkhouse and returned with his brother. They soon began a bucket brigade where they formed a perimeter around the house to prevent the fire from spreading. "Keep on the lookout for cinders flying in the air. Stomp them out as soon as you see one!" Lance coughed after speaking but continued to work with the boys. Soon, Zachariah joined them, and one man worked with a boy at each pump.

They worked until the house had burned itself to hot ashes, and the risk of fire abated. "We were fortunate there was no breeze tonight," Zachariah said as he swiped at his sooty brow. "We could have lost everything."

Lance nodded and whispered, "I almost did."

Zachariah wrapped an arm around each boy's shoulder. "Come rest in my cottage and then go see your mother. Mrs. Wagner is with her, and she'll inform us if she's in any danger."

Simon stepped away from Zachariah and held onto Lance's hand. "You'll get us if Mama..." His lower lip trembled. "Please?"

Lance crouched down and cradled the boy's cheek. "Of course, Simon. But I know your mother will recover. She's strong and brave, just like her boys." He held Simon close as he threw himself into Lance's arms. He looked at Peter and saw him leaning against Zachariah. After a few moments, Simon sniffled and backed away.

"I get the right side of the bed," Peter said, and Simon spun around, his hands on his hips.

"No you don't!" Simon yelled and ran toward Zachariah's small cabin. Peter chased after his brother but didn't run at full speed.

"That was nice of Peter," Zachariah murmured. "To help take Simon's mind off his worry about his mother."

Lance nodded. "They'll be asleep before you get there, and it won't matter which side of the bed they're sleeping on." Lance shared a long look with his boss and friend. "I'll come by with any news, or I'll see you later today."

Lance watched as the foreman walked toward his home, coughing intermittently. Lance took a deep breath and grimaced at the tightness that remained in his own chest. Any personal concerns faded as he thought about Eleanor, and he strode to the bunkhouse. When he arrived, he doffed his hat and ducked his head as he entered. Mrs. Wagner sat beside an ashen Eleanor, although her chest rose and fell with each breath, and her breathing did not seem labored.

"Should we ride for the doctor?" Lance asked.

Mrs. Wagner shook her head. "No, Zachariah asked me that when he brought her here. There's nothin' a doc could do. We must wait and see if she wakes up." She focused on Lance and frowned. "Sit before you fall over, Mr. Gallagher."

He pulled out a chair and sat on the other side of Eleanor's bed. "There's so much I want to tell her," he whispered. "So much I should have said." He reached forward and gripped her hand, raising it so he could kiss it.

Mrs. Wagner made a sound of agreement. "I think you both have regrets about the silence you have kept." She reached forward and softly freed his hand from Eleanor's. "She might not need the doctor, but you do." Mrs. Wagner shook her head in regret at the burns on his hands and the patches where skin had peeled away.

"I'm fine. Our only concern should be Eleanor." He met her challenging gaze.

"No, son, what would she do if she woke and found you ailing and feverish because you let your wounds fester?" She sighed as she looked outside. "I never thought to ask if the root cellar burned."

"No, only the house," Lance said. "Nothing from the house was saved."

"No. Everything that was vital *was* saved," she contradicted him. "Remain here with Eleanor, and I'll be back shortly."

He frowned as he watched her leave. She did not need a lantern as dawn had arrived, and a soft glow lit outside. When the door closed softly behind Mrs. Wagner, Lance rested his head beside Eleanor's hip and let out a stuttering breath. "Oh, Eleanor, what will I do if I lose you, too?" he whispered. "Please, fight. Please come back to us. Your boys need you. And so do I."

He took a long breath, coughing a few times, and raised his head to look at Eleanor. Her chest continued to rise and fall in an easy rhythm, and her face had been cleaned of ash and soot. Her hair, usually so vibrant, had a fine layer of ash dulling the subtle red hue. His hand trembled as he traced a finger over her eyebrow. "Wake, my love," he whispered.

His alert gaze continued to watch her, but she did not awaken at his coaxing. Tears silently leaked down his cheeks. "For I do love you. I've loved you and your boys for longer than I realized." He gripped her hand. "That's what Zachariah and I were speaking about when you came into the barn. He's a good friend, Ellie, and wouldn't betray a confidence. I know you appreciate that about him."

He waited for any sort of response from her, and, when none came, he began to ramble, uncaring what he shared as long as he spoke. "I want you to hear my voice when you waken," he whispered. He told her about sitting by the creek before deciding to return to tell her how he felt.

He ignored Mrs. Wagner returning to the bunkhouse. He paid little attention to her ministrations as she washed his hands and then covered them in a salve she had stored in the root cellar. When she bound them in clean cotton that had been stored in the barn, he nodded his thanks but never interrupted his one-sided conversation with Eleanor. Mrs. Wagner rested on a nearby mattress, but Lance continued to keep his vigil next to Eleanor, insistent to greet her the moment she woke.

CHAPTER 7

Two days later, Doc Gracie had come and gone, and Eleanor remained unconscious in the bunkhouse. Lance and Zachariah had decided to bunk together in Zachariah's foreman's cabin and had turned the bunkhouse into a home for the Ferguson family and Mrs. Wagner, until a new ranch house could be built. Zachariah hoped to build the ranch house in the same general vicinity as the old home but knew they needed to wait for the embers to fully cool before moving the boards and initiating cleanup of the ruined house.

A few minutes ago, a group of men had arrived from town. They had heard the news of the fire after Gracie's return to Rattlesnake Ridge, and Jack Hollis had ridden out with them. Although Lance had resisted Zachariah's summon to join the men outside, he gave in when Zachariah waited for him in the doorway. Lance kissed Eleanor on the forehead and left Eleanor's side with Mrs. Wagner quietly knitting beside her.

Jack, Zachariah, and Lance watched as the townsmen kicked at the rubble, turning over pieces of wood and shaking their heads at the sight of the home reduced to ashes. A few of the men carried buckets of water in case it was necessary, but they had yet to find a hot spot to be put out.

"What a disaster," Jack muttered as he stared at the men wandering around. "Any idea how it started?" He looked first to Zachariah and then to Lance.

Zachariah shook his head. "No. I woke to the sound of Simon screaming from Peter's window." His eyes shone with regret and horror. "By the time I got outside, the house was already half burned." He traced at a healing burn on his left forearm and took a deep breath as though he were again breathing in the smoke-filled air that had welcomed him as he burst into the house in an attempt to save the boys.

"Thank God you went upstairs when you did to save the boys," Lance murmured as he watched Peter and Simon play with their puppy. "And Patch."

"I couldn't find Eleanor," Zachariah whispered,

his voice laced with regret. "I got the boys out and went back inside, but I couldn't find her." He looked at Lance. "I promise you that I did."

Lance nodded. "You couldn't have known she'd be in the kitchen. Thankfully Mrs. Wagner did."

Jack frowned. "How did Mrs. Wagner get out?"

Zachariah shrugged, and Lance spoke up. "She told me, when she opened her bedroom door, the kitchen was like an inferno. She slammed her door shut and climbed out her window. Her room was on the first floor, so she didn't have far to fall."

Jack squinted as though envisioning the scene.

"She also told me that Eleanor had been nursing a cup of tea at the kitchen table as she hadn't planned to go to bed that night," Lance said.

Zachariah gave a grunt as though that made sense and then sighed. "Thank heavens she was not upstairs."

Lance shuddered. "I wish we knew what caused the fire."

Jack shook his head. "It would take a miracle to discover what did. Just as a miracle spared the rest of your buildings." He looked around and shook his head in wonder. "I can't believe at the end of a dry summer that you only lost the house."

"We were fortunate it was a still night," Lance

said. "If there had been any wind..." He cleared his throat. "I fear the house would have burned faster, and we might have lost..." He shook his head, unable to give voice to his worst fear.

Jack murmured his agreement. "Give thanks for all you have and that what was lost can be rebuilt." He frowned as he looked down the lane and saw Sterling Hayden cantering toward them. "It will be interesting to see what he has to say."

Zachariah seemed to bristle, but then he forced himself to relax. "Sterling," he said in his deep voice, little friendliness in his tone.

"I must see her! How is she?" Sterling gasped as he vaulted off his horse. He threw his reins at Lance and glared at him when Lance failed to grab them. "Boy, that is your job. Take care of my horse."

Lance held up his injured hands and shook his head. "I beg your pardon, sir. I'm unable to tend your horse at this time." Although his words could have been construed as meek, his tone verged on hostile.

Sterling grabbed the reins and tied his horse to a paddock rail. "Well, where is Eleanor? I must see her. I must ensure she is well." He swiped at his brow, and his eyes were filled with an ill-defined emotion.

Jack took a step forward, his gaze alert as he studied the man. "Why are you keen on seeing Mrs.

Ferguson? She has her family around her as she heals. Doc Gracie said she should not be bothered by visitors right now."

Sterling puffed out his chest and placed a hand on his burgundy silk waistcoat. "I am not a simple visitor. I am her betrothed."

Zachariah choked and Lance blanched. "Does she know that?" Zachariah asked. When Sterling flushed, Zachariah marched toward the man and used his height in an attempt to intimidate him. "You'd use her incapacitation to force her hand?"

Sterling tilted his head upward in defiance. "It's what she wants. You know how women are. They don't know their minds."

Lance hissed in pain as his injured hands formed fists. "You are a fool. She's been smart enough to outwit you for two years. She'll never agree to marry you."

Sterling glared at Lance and shook his head. "Who are you to have an opinion? You're a ranch hand." He looked at Zachariah. "And you're the foreman. This matter is between your betters."

Jack gripped Lance's arm before he could lunge for the pompous man. "I'd remind you, Sterling, that you are threatening a good woman's reputation." When Sterling snorted at that, Jack shook his head.

"Don't bait them any more than you have. For you won't like the consequences, and I will turn a blind eye."

"You're a man of the law. You have to protect me," Sterling protested.

Jack took a deep breath. "You are acting without honor, and that I will not condone." He nodded to Zachariah and Lance, turned on his heel, and walked away as though to supervise the men who continued to clear away the rubble.

Zachariah leaned forward and whispered in a lethal voice, "I'd leave now, Sterling. Leave before we have a reason to do you harm."

Sterling looked from Zachariah to Lance, who now stood at Zachariah's side. "I have every right to see her."

"No, you have every right to request to see her. And that has been denied," Lance said. "Leave while you can still ride your horse."

Sterling glared at the two men. He stomped to his horse and heaved himself on it before galloping away.

Lance let out a deep breath as he watched the man leave. "I wish I'd been able to punch him."

Zachariah let out a laugh. "Me too. Even though Jack said he wouldn't interfere, it wouldn't have been a good idea. Not with all those witnesses willing to gossip in town." He nodded to the interested stares of the men working on the charred remains of the house.

Lance tilted his head in the direction of the avid stares of Eleanor's sons. "And not in front of the boys."

Peter and Simon raced toward them. They had sat on a distant paddock rail while they talked with Jack and then Sterling Hayden.

"Mr. Lance! Mr. Lance!" Simon gasped as he ran.

"Is Mama really marrying that man?" Peter asked, earning a push from his brother for asking his question.

Lance scratched behind his ear and shrugged. "I believe that man is mistaken, but the only person who can tell us that is your mother. We must wait for her to wake up and tell us."

Simon's bottom lip trembled, and he bit it. "She will wake up?" he asked in a tiny voice.

Lance crouched down and gripped the boy's shoulder. He looked from him to Peter, his gaze earnest and truthful. "I pray she will, but I won't lie to you and assure you that she will. We must never lose hope."

Simon sniffled and fought back tears that wanted to fall.

Peter looked from Lance to Zachariah and slung his arm around his brother's shoulder. "We have no family if Mama dies." He stiffened his shoulders as though to ward off the terror expressed in those words.

"You have family, Peter," Zachariah said. He looked to Peter's younger brother. "Simon. You have me. You have Mrs. Wagner. You have Mr. Lance. And you still have your mama."

Peter nodded and then urged Simon to race him to the sentry tree. The two boys ran off as quickly as they had arrived.

"They're terrified," Zachariah murmured as he watched them run away and play as though they were normal boys without a care in the world. "Mrs. Wagner tells me that they cry themselves to sleep at night and that nothing calms them."

Lance sighed. "Until Eleanor wakes, nothing will."

A soft voice permeated the profound silence, and she strained to hear the words. She tried to open her eyes, but they felt like they were sewn shut. She moved her hand, and the voice stopped speaking. *Keep talking to me*, she thought as the voice was melodic and soothing. Soon she felt hands tracing over her, and she tried to speak.

"El," Zachariah said, and a hand brushed hair off her forehead. "El, wake up."

"Trying," she whispered, uncertain if she spoke or thought the words. When she heard gasps and a sob, she realized she must have spoken. "So hard."

"You can do it, Mama!" her youngest son, Simon, said. She felt his small hand grip her arm as he leaned against her. "We've missed you, Mama."

"Please, Mama," Peter whispered.

She took a deep breath and forced her eyes open. She blinked once and then again to see Simon to her right, Peter on her left, with Zachariah behind him. At the foot of the bed stood Lance and Mrs. Wagner. "Hello," she croaked. "Water, please?"

Mrs. Wagner bustled over to the small kitchen area and returned with a glass as Zachariah helped her sit up. She took a sip of water, sighing with pleasure as it eased the burning dryness in her throat. "Thank you."

Reaching out, she gripped each of her son's hands. "Why are you concerned? I am fine." Her eyes fluttered closed a moment, and she forced them open again. "I'm merely tired."

"You've been asleep for four days," Lance said in a gruff tone. Her gaze met his, and she frowned in confusion.

"I don't understand. Why would I be asleep for that long?" She tugged Simon to her, and he crawled onto the bed to lie beside her. Peter did the same, and she soon cradled both of her boys next to her. "What happened?"

Zachariah cleared his throat. "There was a fire. The ranch house burned." He met her shocked stare. "Nothing is left."

"What about the barn and paddock?" she whispered as she looked around, belatedly realizing she was not in her bedroom but in the bunkhouse.

"Saved," Lance said. "Good to see you've recovered, Miss Eleanor." He nodded at her and slipped from the room.

"I don't understand," she murmured. "How did the house burn?" She kissed her boys on their heads. "I don't remember anything."

Zachariah sat on a chair beside her bed while Mrs. Wagner brewed tea and hummed a song she used to sing when she was content while cooking at her large stove in the ranch house. "Jack was here, and I fear it will always remain a mystery why the house burned. Perhaps a candle overturned." He shrugged. "It's impossible to say."

Her hold on her boys tightened. "How did we survive?"

"I was able to rescue the boys from upstairs, and Mrs. Wagner jumped out of her bedroom window." Zachariah ducked his head and flushed as though he were embarrassed or ashamed.

"And Mr. Lance dunked himself under the water pump before racin' into the house to find you and save you, Mama!" Simon said in his excited voice. "He saved you." His small arms wrapped firmly around her waist, and he buried his head into her side.

"Shh, little love, I am fine," she murmured. "Tired and sore, but fine." She looked at Zachariah. "I have no memory of what happened. How can that be?"

Mrs. Wagner approached with a *tsk* and urged her to sit. "Come, sit up and drink some tea. This will help the aches and ensure you continue to improve." She watched as Eleanor pushed herself up until she sat propped against the pillows. Her boys remained at her side.

Eleanor took a long swallow of the tea and grimaced. "That's terribly bitter."

Mrs. Wagner looked at her unrepentantly. "There is little honey left, and we've not been to town for supplies. Be thankful Doc Gracie left willow bark, or there'd be nothing to help soothe you now."

Eleanor smiled weakly in agreement and took another sip before handing the cup back to Mrs. Wagner. "Did Doc say if I had a head injury?"

Zachariah shook his head. "She could find no reason why you weren't waking up. You were in the smoke a long time." He shared a long look with her but refrained from saying more as he nodded to the boys in her arms.

"Well, I'll be fine now," she whispered. "What... How did Lance return?"

Zachariah shook his head. "That's for you to ask him." He rose. "I'll leave you to have time with your boys."

Eleanor watched him leave and then focused on her boys. "How are you both?" Her grip on them tightened again as she fought images of what could have happened to her precious sons.

"We're fine, Mama," Peter said. He sat up and moved to the chair Zachariah had vacated, although he continued to hold her hand. "As long as you are better, we are fine."

"Have you been minding Zachariah and Mrs.

Wagner?" she asked as she stroked a hand over Peter's forehead and pushed back a lock of his hair.

He smiled and nodded. "Yes. And Mr. Lance made us work extra hard. Since he hurt his hands, he can't do the work he'd like. So we do it for him."

"He hurt his hands?" She frowned as she looked from one son to the other.

Simon shrugged as he played with a loose string on her dress. "He scorched them when he saved you from the fire. Doc Gracie gave us salve to put on his burns, and he has to keep them covered and dry for a while. Can't do no... any heavy lifting." He corrected his language as though Lance were there to scold him.

"I had no idea," she whispered. "I must thank him."

"He says he won't leave, Mama," Simon said, his voice betraying his fear. "But will you make him go away again?"

"Shh, that's not a concern to worry about now," she soothed. "Mr. Gallagher and I have much to discuss."

Peter frowned and looked at his mother with confusion. He seemed to have grown into a young man while she slept, and she silently mourned the loss of her son's innocence. "Is part of your discussion about your agreement to marry Mr. Hayden?"

"What?" Eleanor gasped. She gaped at her son and then met Mrs. Wagner's worried gaze as she sat in a corner in the room. "What a preposterous notion. Who would say such a thing?"

"Mr. Hayden," Peter said.

"I thought Mr. Lance would give him a facer!" Simon said with glee. "I wish he had," he whispered.

"So do I," his mother muttered as she kissed his head. She shook her head in confusion. "I've only ever rebuffed his advances toward me. I have no interest, now or ever, in marrying the man."

"He seemed convinced you'd want to marry him," Mrs. Wagner said. "Even I heard his proclamation from in here."

Eleanor shuddered. "The only way I'd marry him is if I were unconscious and unaware of what I was doing." She shook her head and then laughed. "I wish I could have seen Zachariah react."

Peter grinned as Simon giggled. "He loomed over him, Mama, and scared the dickens out of Mr. Hayden!"

"The deputy would not have been pleased to have such violence occur," Eleanor said. She admonished her boys, "Violence is never the solution."

"Mr. Hollis didn't care if Zachariah and Mr. Lance beat him to a pulp. Turned his back on what was going on and said he wouldn't come to Mr. Hayden's rescue," Simon said with glee.

"Oh my," Eleanor whispered.

"There are those who still need reassurance that Mr. Hayden spoke lies," Mrs. Wagner said. She nodded as Eleanor flushed.

Simon peered up at her, his blue eyes shining with curiosity. "Do you think you might marry again though, Mama? Some other man?"

She flushed and kissed the top of his head. "We'll see." She looked at Peter and squeezed his hand. "Thank you for taking such good care of your brother."

"We took care of each other, Mama, just like you taught us to," Peter said.

She kissed Simon's head again and pulled Simon close so she could kiss his cheek. "You are precious, my little loves." She rested for many minutes with her sons nearby as she considered the conversation to come.

L ance pulled out his bedroll and slung it over his shoulder. Although the nights had begun to cool now that it was mid-September, he needed time alone. Zachariah was not an overly talkative roommate, but Lance feared Zachariah would have much to say this evening. Lance ensured Amaretto was settled and slipped from the barn. The sound of laughter trickled out of the bunkhouse, and he smiled as he envisioned the tales Simon and Peter told their mother. With a sigh, and a pang of longing, he turned to walk up the hill to find a comfortable place to pitch his bedroll.

After walking a short distance, he found a place on the apex of a hill where he could see the ranch. After unfurling his bedroll, he sat and contemplated the day's events. "Ellie," he murmured as he thought about seeing Eleanor's bright blue eyes again. Their brilliance had been dulled when she first woke, but then the sparkle slowly returned as she fully returned to them.

He plucked a piece of prairie grass and twirled it between his fingers. When he stood at the foot of the bed, watching her hug and reassure her boys that she was well, he yearned for just such an embrace. However, she had spared him barely a glance, and he'd keenly felt the absence of her regard.

"Perhaps I should have stayed," he muttered as he rubbed at his head. With a sigh, he flopped backward onto his bedroll and stared at the stars overhead. He raised an arm as he tried to determine the constellations shining in the sky overhead and then dropped it to his side as he fought a quiet ache. His wife, Amy, had known the constellations and had enjoyed teaching them to him. Letting out a deep breath, he realized this was the first time he'd searched for constellations since her death. His eyes pricked with unshed tears as he mourned the life he would never have with Amy and their daughter.

After a moment, a sense of peace filled him as he felt no guilt in loving Eleanor. Amy would want him to find another to love. She would want him to be happy again. As he stared at the stars, he gave thanks at having the chance at creating a life with Eleanor. He hoped she would welcome the gift of a second chance that had been granted to them. An owl hooted, and he sat up and stared down at the ranch in the distance. Tonight, Eleanor needed time with her family. Tomorrow, they would talk.

CHAPTER 8

The following morning, Eleanor had bathed and was in a clean nightgown Gracie had brought out to the ranch. Gracie had had the foresight to bring a set of clothes for her and the boys when she visited again yesterday after Eleanor had awoken. She rubbed at her forehead and then smoothed a hand over her clean hair, sniffing with distaste at the faint scent of smoke that clung to her locks.

"Why the disgust?" Lance asked from the doorway.

She flushed and dropped her hand to hold on her lap. "I wish I still didn't smell like a fireplace."

His eyes flashed with regret and fear as he looked at her. "Be thankful, Ellie," he rasped. He ducked his head at the use of his nickname for her. "I beg your pardon."

"Ellie?" she whispered. "No one's ever called me Ellie before."

When he met her inquisitive gaze, he made sure his was shuttered, and he stood with impeccable posture. "Forgive me for returning when you asked me to leave."

She rolled her eyes and motioned for him to enter the room. "I would be dead if you hadn't returned, Lance. Mrs. Wagner has told me that so many times since I woke up." She paused as she stared at him with a touch of wonder. "You returned."

"I did," he whispered and then cleared his throat. "Sterling Hayden visited while you were unwell."

Her eyes flashed with annoyance, and she gripped her hands together on her lap. "I know. The boys asked me if I was going to marry him." She saw Lance tense as he waited for her to speak. "I'm not. I never gave him any encouragement."

"Good." The tenseness in his shoulders eased as his gaze roved over her.

She bit her lip as he remained standing beside her bed and said nothing further. "I was distraught to know you'd already departed."

"What?" he asked, his eyes flashing with curiosity and surprise.

"Will you sit?" She peered up at him. "I don't care to add a crick in my neck to the list of things that ache." They shared a brief smile, and he sat without touching her.

"After supper that night, the night I asked you to leave, I sought you out. I didn't really want you to go." She watched him with wide luminous eyes, and the hope in her gaze faded as he watched her impassively. "Say something."

He stared at her a long moment and then murmured, "What would you have said to me had I still been in the barn?"

She flushed and gripped her hands together. "I would have admitted I'd been a fool." She looked at him pleadingly and then continued, "I would have asked you to stay."

"Why?" he whispered, his gaze no long impassive. It shone with passionate intensity as he stared at her.

As she met his gaze, she relaxed. "Because I wanted you to stay. I can't imagine the ranch without you here." She swallowed. "I...I want you here."

He reached forward with bandaged hands and

brushed a wisp of hair off her cheek. "What are you saying?"

"Was it a dream when I fought to regain consciousness?" She seemed to gather her courage as he shook his head in confusion. "You called me *your love*. You professed your love for me. Did I dream that?"

"No," he said in a low voice. "I love you. I have for some time." He cupped her face and leaned toward her. "I...Why would you want a ranch hand?"

She made a scoffing noise and turned her face to kiss his bandaged palm. "You are beloved, Lance." Her voice broke as tears leaked out. "I almost lost you to my pride and stubbornness." She sniffled. "I love you, so very much."

"Eleanor," he rasped as he rested his forehead against hers. "My Ellie." He looked at her. "I know I don't have much to offer, but my hands will heal, and I will work hard to help you rebuild the ranch house. I will do everything I can to help you have a successful ranch."

"Do you want to run it?" she asked.

"Only with you," he said, and he smiled as her eyes brightened. "Marry me, Ellie."

She ran her hands through his thick blond hair, her smile brilliant and her eyes shining with happiness. "Yes, my Lance. My beloved. Yes." She met his kiss and then held him close as he hugged her.

"I've never been so afraid in all my life," he whispered into her hair as he ran his hands over her back. "When I thought you were upstairs, and the stairway was filled with flames...I couldn't have reached you."

"*Shh*," she soothed. "I'm fine now."

He shook his head and leaned away, his eyes tear-brightened. "I swore, after Amy and Laura died, I swore that I'd never love again. That I'd never risk hurting like that again." He looked at her with wonder. "I never expected to find you."

She laughed and traced a finger over his cheek, her thumb running over and around his dimple. "Do you believe after all I lived through with Alan that I ever expected to love again? To trust another man again? To ever consider marrying again?" Her eyes filled, and she studied him. "I never thought I would be able to. You proved me wrong."

He pulled her close. "Oh, Eleanor, we will have the most wonderful life. You, me, and the boys."

She sobbed as he held her, and he loosened his hold. "Forgive me," he whispered.

"No," she said as she grabbed his hand to prevent him from moving away from her. "It's a miracle to me how much you care for them, too. I never thought...I never thought another man would care for them as though they were his own."

Lance's eyes shone as he made her a vow. "I do, Ellie. I could never love them any more than I already do. They are wonderful boys, and I would be proud to call them my sons."

She nodded as tears leaked out. "Yes."

"We will have a beautiful life together," he whispered.

"Yes," she said again as she hugged him one last time before Mrs. Wagner returned.

Three days later, Eleanor was up and about and helping to oversee the transformation of the bunkhouse into a small home for her family. The large room for the men had been partitioned into two small rooms. The boys had their own space, and she and Mrs. Wagner shared a room. The kitchen area had been expanded to hold a table. Although small, Eleanor knew they would be fine.

She decided to take a break after the bedrooms were arranged and sat on one of the rocking chairs on the front porch. Smiling, she watched as Lance worked with Peter and Simon. The boys exulted at the news that Lance and she were to marry. She sighed as she looked back at the small bunkhouse as she didn't know when the marriage would take place with such cramped living quarters. She frowned when she saw Simon look down the lane and then race toward her.

"Mama, Mama, Mama!" he yelled as he careened toward her.

She opened her arms and caught him so he would not fall. "Yes, my little love?" she asked as he panted from his mad dash from the paddock.

"Mr. Hayden is about to arrive," Simon said.

"Oh my," Eleanor breathed as she rose. She placed a hand on Simon's shoulder for a moment, but he squirmed to be free and raced away again just as Sterling's horse trotted into the yard. She raised a hand over her eyes and shook her head at Lance who walked in her direction. Lance stopped in his tracks and watched from a distance as Sterling approached her.

After Sterling dismounted, he tied his horse to a paddock rail and walked in her direction, ignoring Lance and her boys. When he reached her, he doffed his hat and reached for her hand. When she moved in a way to prevent him from clasping her hand, he frowned. "My dearest Mrs. Ferguson," he murmured. "I am most relieved to see you much improved."

"Are you?" she asked with one eyebrow raised. "I should have thought it would better serve your purposes were I to have remained unconscious."

He frowned and shook his head in confusion at her words. "I fear you may still be recovering from your illness for you have no idea what you are saying."

"I assure you, Mr. Hayden, I am in complete control of my faculties, and I am well aware of what I say. And I mean what I say." Her eyes flashed with annoyance as he looked at her as a father would a recalcitrant child.

"My dear Mrs. Ferguson," he began again, fighting a glare when she shook her head in disagreement. "I was most concerned about your well-being. They would not allow me to see you the last time I visited."

"I was in no condition to see anyone. Only the doctor visited me," she said. When he took a step closer to her, she backed away a step. "I thank you for your concern, sir, but, as you can see, I am recovered and well taken care of by my family."

"That's just it," he said in a low voice that grated

on her nerves. "I want to be family. I want to care for you."

Her eyes flashed with annoyance and resentment. "Is that why you lied to Mr. Gallagher and Mr. O'Neill, informing them we were betrothed?" She waited for a rebuttal or denial but watched as he gaped at her. "For you know as well as I do that I never accepted you."

He quickly recovered his composure and smiled with as much charm as he could muster. "That is a mere formality between those who care for each other as you and I do. For we've known for some time that the only future for us is wedded bliss. Is that not so, Mrs. Ferguson?"

She rolled her eyes and shook her head. "No, that is not what I foresee. For I do not care for you. Not in that manner and I will not marry a man I do not love."

He scoffed and looked at her as though she were a naïve girl still playing with dolls. "Who needs love when we could establish a formidable ranching empire?"

"You have no idea, do you?" she whispered as she looked at him with blatant pity. "For if you do not have love, then none of it is worthwhile. Not the number of cattle, not the masses of acres, none of it."

He flushed red and leaned toward her. "To speak to me in such a manner, I assume you imagine yourself in love with another."

"Yes," she said, refusing to back away as he towered over her. "Although it is not my imaginings. It is the truth."

Sterling looked over the ranch with a covetous stare and then at her with a gaze filled with scorn. "Whoever he is, he only wants you for your ranch. Never for you. Who would want to be saddled with two boys who aren't his?"

"I would," Lance said in a strong voice behind Sterling.

Sterling spun around so quickly he almost fell to the ground at Lance's voice. "You have no right to interrupt my conversation with your boss. I would assume you have duties to attend to, although, with your injuries, I imagine you are a rather worthless hand. If you worked for me, I'd have fired you by now."

"Then I shall remain ever thankful I refused your offer of employment and continued here to inquire for work," Lance murmured as he stared at Sterling.

"What?" Eleanor gasped as she looked at the two men glaring at each other.

Lance spoke to Eleanor, although his gaze never

left that of Sterling's. "On the day I arrived, I passed him on the road. He attempted to entice me to work for him rather than you, but I declined."

Sterling growled. "You were after an easy mark."

Lance stiffened, and his hands fisted. "I'd watch your tongue. You're insulting my betrothed, and I will have no remorse in teaching you manners."

Sterling spun to glare at Eleanor. "You can't be serious? You aren't going to marry this... this...laborer?"

Eleanor beamed at him. "I am. And I know we will be quite happy."

Lance shared a long stare with the man. "Your visits to the Broken Pine are no longer required. And you should know, your interference in the ranch will no longer be tolerated."

Sterling shook his head in confusion. "I don't know what you mean." He puffed out his chest and appeared insulted as he thought through Lance's words. "I hope you are not implying I had anything to do with the unfortunate destruction of the ranch house?"

Lance shook his head. "No, but there have been other suspicious events. You'd do well to inform those who work for you that any mischief will not be taken lightly."

Sterling slammed his hat on and marched away, not bothering to wish Eleanor a good day. He mounted his horse and cantered away before pushing his horse to a gallop.

Eleanor let out a sigh and slipped her arm through Lance's, leaning against his side. "I wonder if he will accept your warning and rethink his visits."

"The man isn't stupid, Ellie," Lance said as he kissed the top of her head. "He'll stay away because he understands you're not alone now." He shrugged. "You never were. You always had Zachariah. But, for a man like Sterling, until you committed yourself to another man, you were open to a relationship with him. Now he knows you aren't."

She smiled as she pressed herself more closely to his side. "And he knows you are competent and able to work the ranch with Zachariah. He's not fool-hardy enough to challenge you."

He chuckled and hugged her closer. "Thank you for your confidence in me." He held her for a few minutes before kissing her on the forehead and returning to work with the boys.

On Sunday, they traveled into town for church and the fall church picnic to be held after the service. Eleanor had little to offer after the fire, and she had informed the boys their contribution was helping to serve and to clean up. Eleanor rode next to Lance in the wagon while Zachariah rode his favorite horse, Rogue. The boys chattered the entire trip into town, excited to see their friends and to tell them the tale of the fire.

"No embellishments, boys," Lance said as he shared a smile with Eleanor.

Simon sat on his knees behind them, waving his arms about. "But, Mr. Lance, the flames, and the windows blowing open, and you running into our burning house." He paused when Lance made a noise in his throat.

Eleanor shuddered next to Lance and gripped his arm. "Mr. Lance is correct, Simon. No embellishing. From everything you've told me, there is no need for it." She looked at her two sons in the only clothes they had. "The truth will still be enough to shock your friends."

She sighed as Peter and Simon settled down behind them in the wagon bed to talk over what they wanted to say to their friends. "I should have known they'd want to regale their friends with the house inferno," she said in a low voice to Lance.

He gripped her hand for a moment. "It's natural for them to tell their friends. The more they talk about it, the less fear they'll have." He smiled at her. "I've found silence often makes a fear grow."

She leaned into his side. "How true," she murmured. She smiled at acquaintances and friends as they arrived at the church, accepting a hand down from Lance. She walked into the church on his arm, ignoring the curious stares as her boys walked behind her with Zachariah.

After the service, Eleanor stood beside Lance with her arm through his. She had already spoken to Barbara and Gracie, and word had leaked that she and Lance were engaged. Although she had tried to help with the preparations for the church picnic, the townsfolk continued to approach her and Lance to congratulate them, making it impossible to aid with the setup.

"Congratulations," Mayor Jacob Winthrop said as he paused to speak with them. "I'm delighted to hear the news. For your happiness and for the stability of your ranch." Winthrop was an astute businessman, but he also wanted to ensure his town flourished and attracted new residents.

"Thank you, Mr. Winthrop," Eleanor said. "May I introduce my fiancé, Lance Gallagher?"

Winthrop seemed to take Lance's measure as he shook Lance's hand. "You're earning a reputation as a competent rancher."

Lance nodded. "I do my best, sir."

Winthrop focused on Eleanor. "It's a darned shame what happened to your house."

She nodded, her grip on Lance's arm tightening. "Yes, but we all survived. That is what matters."

"Yes, it is." He tipped his hat to the couple and moved on, allowing others to offer their congratulations. By the time they had finished speaking with the townsfolk, the tables were laden with food, and most townsfolk had a plate in their hands.

"Seems we're too late to help," Eleanor said.

Lance smiled reassuringly at her. "They are happy to see you well. They don't begrudge you anything." He kissed her forehead as she slipped her arm free to speak with Barbara and Gracie while he joined Zachariah and Jack.

She hugged her friends and fought her inclination to squeal like a schoolgirl with delight at her situation. "Thank you for spreading the rumor," she whispered to her friends. "I couldn't have handled the speculative glances if they thought I was having a dalliance with Lance."

Eleanor smiled in a noncommittal way as the reporter's wife, Beth Langhorne, approached them. "Hello, Mrs. Langhorne."

Beth smiled and sipped at her punch. "Hello. I wanted to offer my congratulations and inform you that, when you do wed, Samuel and I would be pleased to run an announcement of that blessed event in the paper. It will then be posted at the General Store for all to see."

Eleanor smiled. "That is most kind. However, I fear it may be some time until we wed. The living arrangements are rather cramped at the moment at the ranch, and I would prefer to wait until I feel more settled."

Beth sobered. "I can't begin to imagine what you suffered." She waited for Eleanor to respond and then sighed at the ensuing silence. "Again, I offer my congratulations." She smiled at the small group of women and walked away.

Barbara watched Beth Langhorne mingle with other churchgoers, never remaining long in any group's company. "Everyone's afraid of saying something that will end up printed in the paper."

Eleanor sighed. "I'd think she'd be lonely."

Gracie shrugged. "Perhaps she is. But I believe she is quite happy with her husband." She paused before speaking as she heard a snippet of gossip, frowning as the words were carried on the soft breeze.

"I tell you, it's a disgrace she's marrying another. She should marry that foreman and legitimize that boy once and for all," the woman said in an imperious tone.

"Is that…?" Eleanor asked as she stiffened.

"Yes, Mrs. Handley," Barbara said as she glared in the direction of the voice. "Oh my," she breathed, causing Eleanor and Gracie to look in that direction.

Adeline Brown, the preacher's wife, approached Mrs. Handley with a purposeful stride. Adeline looked like a general about to marshal troops, and Eleanor instinctively stood a little taller as she watched Adeline. "Mrs. Handley," the preacher's wife said in a no-nonsense voice. "I am most displeased with the rumors I have heard circulating at your fine store."

Mrs. Handley flushed and shook her head in feigned confusion. "I'm afraid I have no idea what you are talking about.

"Have you or have you not said on more than one occasion that Mrs. Ferguson knows no shame and

RAMONA FLIGHTNER

should be shunned due to her mistreatment of her deceased husband?"

Mrs. Handley gaped as her mouth opened and closed numerous times while no sound emerged.

"Have you not intimated that any upstanding woman in this town must shun her or be tainted by her supposed indiscretion?"

Mrs. Handley raised her chin in defiance of Mrs. Brown's words, although her friends slunk away like cockroaches exposed to sunlight.

"I expect you to call for tea Tuesday at 2 p.m." She waited a moment until Mrs. Handley nodded her agreement before she spun on her heel and returned to her husband's side.

Barb hid her delight by taking a sip of punch and then turned away as Mrs. Handley slipped into the shadows. "That should help rid any ongoing suspicions." She smiled at her friend. "What I wouldn't give to be at that tea on Tuesday."

Eleanor burst out laughing. "I agree. And I find I'm no longer as affected by her malicious words." She gripped her friend's arm. "I almost died, Barb. After something like that, gossip isn't important." Her smile broadened. "And I reconciled with Lance."

Barbara gave a knowing nod. "Yes, once we find love and face our fears, we realize what is and isn't important." She looked in the direction of her husband and gave an appreciative sigh. "I can say, we are most fortunate to have fallen in love with such attractive men."

Eleanor nodded. "Yes, but more than that, such good men." She walked arm and arm with Barbara to join Jack and Lance and to enjoy the church picnic.

Three days later, Simon gave a shout as he acted as sentinel in the old pine. Lance looked up from working on the bunkhouse roof as he wanted to ensure it was secure for the upcoming winter. He scratched at his head and rubbed at the sweat on his brow when he looked down the drive with a perplexed frown. "What the devil?" he asked as he walked to the ladder and climbed down.

"Mr. Lance!" Simon hollered from the tree. "Do you see?" He gave a *whoop* of delight and clambered out of the branches as he raced to stand beside Lance. Peter emerged from the barn where he'd been working with Zachariah, and they stood in a row as a line of wagons laden with lumber rolled into the yard. Men on horseback accompanied the wagons, and Jacob Winthrop yelled his hello.

"Good morning!" the mayor called out. "We thought we'd have a good ol' house-raising!"

Lance shook his head as he looked at the assembled men. "I…I don't know what to say." He shared a panicked look with Zachariah.

Jacob jumped from the wagon and approached them. "Consider this the town's wedding gift. We want to do this for Mrs. Ferguson after all the disparaging comments over the years about her husband." He grimaced. "And about her."

Lance smiled. "She'll be delighted." He looked up the lane and saw another wagon approaching, this one filled with women. "Why are they here?"

Jacob laughed and hit him on his shoulder. "To drive us mad with suggestions. And to feed us." He winked at him and Zachariah before calling out to the men about where to start unloading the lumber. After a moment he called over Zachariah and Lance. "Where would you like the new house to be built?"

Lance frowned. "Eleanor should decide." He smiled as he saw her standing on the bunkhouse porch with a hand covering her mouth as she gaped at the spectacle in her barnyard. "Ellie!" he called out and waved for her to join them.

When she approached, she smiled her welcome

to Jacob and moved into Lance's side. "I can't begin to imagine why you're here," she breathed.

"They're building us a new house," Lance said, unable to hide his broad smile. When she gaped at him, he nodded with delight. "Come, where would you like it?" He walked with her as they approached the scarred remains of the old house.

"Near the old house as the privy, root cellar, and water pump are nearby," she murmured. After a moment, she pointed to a spot on the other side of her vegetable garden that sat on a small rise. It would give a good view out to the valley and mountains in the distance. "I always wished the house was up here, but it was built when we won the ranch."

Jacob Winthrop joined them and scratched at his face. "This might seem like a perfect place right now, but, when the winds blow, you won't want to have such an exposed home. It will never be warm, no matter how well we build it." He waited for Eleanor to overcome her disappointment. "How about there?" He pointed to a flat place nearer the root cellar.

Eleanor walked over there and around in the grass. After a moment, she smiled and nodded. "What do you think, Lance?"

He shrugged. "Wherever you want the house is

fine with me." He looked at Jacob. "And, if you have questions about how the house should be built, speak with Ellie. She is the expert in this domain." He kissed Eleanor on her forehead and left to help unload the lumber from the back of the wagons.

As they watched Lance join the lumbermen, Jacob murmured, "Extraordinary. Most men want to have much more control over how things are done."

Eleanor smiled at Jacob Winthrop. "Lance wants me happy. And he doesn't care what the house is like. Only that we'll be married and live in it together." She smiled at the town's mayor. "I can't believe you're doing this for me."

Jacob flushed and looked away from her searching gaze. "The fact is, I fear the townsfolk have not treated you as well as we should have. That we have not shown you the compassion we should have after Alan's death." He met her shocked gaze. "I know that nothing will ever make amends for how you were treated, but I hope this will begin to heal the hurt of what occurred."

She smiled at him as she battled tears. "It does.

Thank you." She looked at the place her home would be built and waved her arms about as she described the home she envisioned. "I know it can't be as grand as the home that burned."

He shook his head and smiled. "I brought the best lumbermen and builders with me. We'll have a new home built for you in no time."

"Thank you, Mr. Winthrop," she said. "I should ensure the women who have traveled here today are comfortable." He tipped his hat at her, and she walked with a measured gait to the townswomen who had traveled here. Barbara stood with her daughter, Isabelle, and Eleanor gave Barbara a welcoming hug. "Thank you for coming," she whispered.

Barbara giggled and nodded to Mrs. Handley. "I wouldn't have missed this for the world."

Eleanor shook her head in confusion. "Why?"

"You'll see," Barbara said with a wink. Barbara pasted on an impersonal smile as Mrs. Handley approached them with a few of the townswomen who had a propensity to gossip.

Mrs. Handley looked as though she had just swallowed half a jar of castor oil as she squared her shoulders and faced Eleanor. "Mrs. Ferguson," she said in her carrying voice. "It has been brought to my attention by an estimable member of our town, Mrs. Brown, that I have wronged you." She paused and then cleared her throat. "I am most sincere in my apology, and I ask for your forgiveness."

Eleanor fought a smile as she watched the shopkeeper squirm. "For what are you asking my forgiveness?"

Mrs. Handley flushed. "For ever imagining that you would act dishonorably. I beg your pardon for ever believing you had strayed from your marriage vows."

"How do you know you were wrong?" Eleanor asked.

Mrs. Handley flushed. "It has been brought to my attention that Zachariah was away from the ranch when you were expecting your second child."

"Yes, he was, although few remember he had to return to Ohio to see his dying mother," Eleanor said. After a moment, she smiled with grim satisfaction. "You were wrong, and your insinuations caused me much consternation. You have my forgiveness because you did not harm my son with your mindless chatter. As far as I know, he remains innocent to your prattle." Her gaze was filled with warning, and Mrs. Handley nodded. Eleanor's smile broadened and became more sincere. "Come, let's celebrate the joy of friendship today."

Eleanor moved to the wagon the women had driven out, her mouth dropping open to see the amount of food the women had brought. However, the true surprise was in the last wagon to arrive. That wagon was chockablock full of items that would fill a home. Chairs, tables, lamps, mattresses. A butter churn and an icebox for the kitchen. She rubbed at her forehead and fought tears. "I...I can never repay such kindnesses," she murmured.

Barbara wrapped an arm around one of her shoulders. "Every time there has been a request for aid, you have found a way to help. Food, clothes, anything. This is everyone's way of thanking you."

Eleanor swiped at her cheeks and took a deep breath. "I thought we'd have to live humbly for a while."

Barbara laughed. "And so you will. It will be some time before you can afford to buy the little luxuries you were used to. But these necessities will help your house feel like a home."

Eleanor worked with Barbara and Isabelle as they set up a trestle table laden with food in the barn's shade for the men's midday meal. After everything was ready, she instructed the men unloading the wagon with items for her home to place them in stalls in the barn. "The horses can remain in the paddock for as long as necessary." Soon, most of the work was done, and she found a shaded spot near the bunkhouse to watch the men work.

She sighed with pleasure as she watched Lance working alongside Zachariah, his lean muscles flexing underneath his shirt. She giggled as Barbara nudged her shoulder. "I'm so fortunate, Barb," she whispered.

"You are," Barbara said as she watched Isabelle race off to play with Peter and Simon. "You didn't squander your chance at happiness. Many would have."

Eleanor fought a shudder. "I almost did." She looked at her friend as Barbara stared at her with curiosity. "I sent him away. And he left." She paused as she watched him tease Zachariah, and then both men laughed. "He returned to me and ran into a burning house to save me."

Barbara fought tears as she gripped Eleanor's hand. "I can't imagine what would have happened if he hadn't."

"I know Zachariah would have tried, but he was already exhausted and ill after saving the boys from upstairs. I fear both of us would have died had he attempted to reenter the house." Eleanor wrapped an arm around her waist and let out a deep breath as she let go of the residual fear and anxiety that lingered every time she thought about what could have happened.

"Focus on your future, Eleanor. Soon you will be married to the man you love."

Eleanor nodded as she watched Lance work. "Yes, soon we will be married."

That evening, Lance leaned against the paddock in the gentle breeze as he stared at the skeleton of the house that would be the home he would share with Eleanor, Peter, and Simon. Lance marveled at all the men had completed in one day, his appreciation for Winthrop's ability to motivate his men growing the longer he was in the man's presence. Lance smiled as Eleanor approached, and he opened his arms to her.

She snuggled into his embrace for a moment before turning to face the construction. He tugged her back against his front, his arms wrapped around her middle. He breathed in her subtle scent and kissed her neck. "There's my Ellie," he murmured and smiled as she giggled.

"It will be a beautiful home," she whispered as she stared at the house.

"It will be because you will live there. I could live in a sodbuster's palace and be happy, as long as I was with you, Ellie, and the boys." He released her when she squirmed against him.

"Truly?" she asked.

He nodded and frowned when he saw doubt in her gaze. "I love this land. I won't deny it. I've always wanted to live on a ranch that prospered." He frowned as he saw his words provoked panic. He cupped her face. "But I will never want anything more than I want you and the boys."

She sighed and leaned into his embrace. "I'm being foolish."

"Tell me," he urged when she remained silent.

"I've allowed Sterling's bitterness to sully our happiness." She felt him stiffen, and she squeezed him with her arms. "He taunted me that you only wanted me for the ranch. That no man would truly want me." She paused. "Especially because I had the boys."

Lance stepped away to again bracket her face with his palms. "I don't know who I fell in love with first. You or your boys. I can't imagine a life without any of you. Please believe me, Ellie."

She smiled at him and nodded. "I do." She frowned as she saw him grimace.

"I haven't been forthright with you," he whispered.

She tilted her head and paled. "What do you mean?" she asked, her eyes rounded with fear.

He gripped her arm to still her erratic movements. "No, Ellie. There's no need for panic." His soothing voice calmed her, and he waited until she stilled. "I have money set aside. From when I sold my homestead." He cleared his throat. "After Amy died, I had no desire to live alone on the ranch I had hoped to share with her and our children. I no longer saw a future there. So I sold it to a man like Sterling. And then I began to drift. I deposited the proceeds in the bank when I arrived in town."

"Why did you never tell me?" she whispered. "Why not buy your own place?"

He shrugged. "It's not enough for a parcel of land with water rights. And without water in Nevada, what's the point?" He looked at her. "Besides, I had promised myself I would drift until I died. I never planned on settling down again." He smiled at her as she leaned into him again. "And then I met you and the boys, and I found my dreams of drifting fading as I was seduced by the promise of a family."

"Oh, Lance," she whispered.

"I want you to know it means your concerns about finances are eased. If the cattle prices remain low this year, we will be fine." He kissed her brow. "We have money to buy another spinning wheel and to replace what was lost in the fire." He held her gaze. "And there is plenty of money for a beautiful wedding dress." He smiled as she flushed.

"As long as there are enough funds for a new suit for the bridegroom," she whispered. He laughed and hauled her close.

"Oh, there are," he said as he hugged her. "I fear I'll run out of patience before the clothes are ready." He continued to hold her as dusk descended and the evening chilled. "Soon, Ellie, soon we will be married."

EPILOGUE

At the end of September, Lance paced at the front of the church as he awaited Eleanor's arrival. Peter and Simon sat on a pew in front of him, tugging at their wedding finery and arguing over who could give him the ring. He shook his head and looked at the boys. "Whatever you do, don't lose it."

Peter's eyes rounded, and he nodded as he grabbed the ring out of Simon's palm. When Simon complained, Lance cleared his throat, and Simon kicked his heels on the floor.

Lance looked at the pews rapidly filling with townsfolk, and he was surprised how many of them he recognized. Some were from the weekly church services. Others he knew from the house raising. He grimaced as he saw Sterling Hayden enter and nodded to the man who sat in a prominent seat in the church. After a moment, he ignored the man and focused on those he had begun to consider friends.

Soon the crowd hushed, and he looked down the aisle. "Ellie," he whispered in awe as he saw her standing beside Zachariah in a cream-colored dress with little ornamentation. She had opted for a simple wedding dress so they could wed sooner. The simplicity of the dress highlighted her natural beauty, and he focused on the joy shining in her eyes. He took a deep breath as he waited for her to slowly walk toward him, his gaze never leaving hers.

"My Ellie," he whispered as he took her hand.

"Lance," she murmured with a bright smile. They turned to face the preacher, although Lance barely heard a word of the service.

After what seemed like two minutes, Reverend Brown asked for the ring. Lance turned to Peter and frowned as the boy looked at him with panic-stricken eyes. "Don't tell me you lost it," Lance whispered.

Peter shook his head and held up his hand where the ring was stuck on his thumb.

Eleanor giggled, and Lance rubbed at his head as

he fought a smile. "I fear the ring is … already in use, sir," Lance murmured.

Reverend Brown furrowed his brow and then smiled broadly as he saw what had occurred. "Aye, I fear you didn't want to misplace the ring, although I doubt you foresaw this happening, did you, lad?" He pursed his lips as he thought and then opened his Bible. "Come, place your hand in the Bible."

Peter gaped at him and then placed his hand inside the opened Bible. The reverend winked at the boy and continued his sermon. He cleared his throat when he got to the part where Lance was to place the ring on Eleanor's finger. "Come." He gripped Peter's hand and motioned for Eleanor to hold it. He then placed Lance's hand over both of theirs. Simon pushed in, wanting to be part of the ceremony, and soon all four of their hands were clasped.

"Seems appropriate," Reverend Brown murmured to the chuckling congregation. He finished the ceremony as Lance stared into Eleanor's eyes, one hand over hers and Peter's, the other cradling Simon's head.

He leaned forward to kiss her after they were pronounced husband and wife, and murmured, "This is how it will always be. We'll always be a family." He kissed her softly and then hugged each of the boys. "Walk down the aisle behind us," he murmured to Peter and Simon and held out his elbow to Eleanor who beamed at the congregation.

Soon they were outside accepting well-wishes from all in attendance except Sterling Hayden who had slipped out of the church after they said their vows. Simon and Peter had run off to play with their friends, and Eleanor had murmured, "Oh my. I hope he doesn't lose the ring."

Lance shook his head in resignation and then focused on the long line of friends who wanted to speak with them. As the line petered out, he saw Mrs. Brown standing beside Peter. She appeared pleased with herself.

"Go ahead, boy," she urged.

Peter opened his fist and held out the ring to Lance. "Mrs. Brown helped me," he said with a grimace.

"Nothing a little soap and water couldn't fix," Mrs. Brown said with a nod. "Come along, there are others waiting to wish them well."

Peter scampered away to play with Ishmael and other friends while Lance slipped the ring onto his wife's finger. "Now I feel as though we are properly married," he said with a contented sigh.

She giggled and leaned into his side. "I will never

forget that ceremony. Thank you for wanting the boys to be part of the ceremony."

He traced a tendril of loose hair along her forehead. "I wouldn't have wanted it any other way."

After they thanked the final guest, he tugged her to the side of the church. She frowned as she knew they were expected at the town hall for a wedding feast. "No," he whispered. "I wanted to say something before we joined the others. Here beside the church." He took a deep breath. "I know we've said our vows in front of the reverend and congregation. But these are my vows to you."

He waited a moment and then said in a deep, true voice, "I vow to always love you. To always ensure your happiness. To work hard every day to see you smile. There is no treasure greater to me than your laughter or your joy or that of the boys' well-being." He kissed her palm. "Thank you for becoming my wife."

Tears coursed down her cheek, and she cupped his face as she stared into his eyes. "I vow to never take your love for granted. To always trust you. And to never let fear overcome my love for you." She smiled at him.

"We will have a wonderful life," he whispered.

"Yes," she breathed as she arched up to meet his kiss. "The most wonderful life."

Want to read more about Lance and Eleanor? Click here for a bonus scene I wrote just for my newsletter subscribers!

WANT TO KNOW WHAT HAPPENS NEXT IN THE SERIES?

Want to know what happens next?

Read Returning From Rhode Island!

Available on Amazon!

NEVER MISS A RAMONA FLIGHTNER UPDATE!

Thank you for reading *Drifting From Deadwood*! I hope you enjoyed Lance and Eleanor's story as much as I enjoyed writing it. Please consider leaving a review! Reviews help other readers take a chance on books, and they mean the world to me. Thank you!

I love hearing from you, so please feel free to write me and let me know what you think!

You can reach me at: ramona@ramonaflightner.com

Join My Newsletter For Updates, Bonus Scenes, and Sneak Peeks about the series you love!

Want new release alerts, access to bonus materials

and exclusive giveaways, and all my announcements first? Subscribe to my weekly newsletter!

Want to be notified about freebies and sales? Try Bookbub!

Want to stay up to date on new releases, my life in beautiful Montana, and research trip adventures? Follow my hashtag #ramonasmontanalife to follow along with my adventures as I post gorgeous pictures and videos of my life in Montana. Find Me On Facebook! Or Find Me On Instagram!

ALSO BY RAMONA FLIGHTNER

The O'Rourke Family Montana Saga

Never fear, I am busy at work on the next book in the series! If you want to make sure you never miss a release, a special, a cover reveal, or a short story just for my fans, sign up for my newsletter!

Follow the O'Rourke Family as they settle in Fort Benton, Montana Territory in 1860 and 1870's.

Sign up here to receive the prequel, *Pioneer Adventure* to the new Saga as a thank you for subscribing to my newsletter!

Pioneer Adventure (Prequel)

Pioneer Dream (OFMS, Book 1)- Kevin and Aileen

Pioneer Desire- (OFMS, Book 2)- Ardan and Deirdre

Pioneer Yearning- (OFMS, Book 3) Niamh and Cormac

Pioneer Longing (OFMS, Book 4)- Eamon and Phoebe

Pioneer Bliss (OFMS, Book 5) Declan and Lorena

Pioneer Devotion (OFMS, Book 6) Maggie and Dunmore-

Pioneer Ardor (OFMS, Book 7) Lucien and Samantha

Pioneer Redemption (OFMS, Book 8) Finn and Winnifred

Pioneer Delight (OFMS, Book 9) Niall and Henrietta

Pioneer Valor (OFMS, Book 10) Oran and Olivia

Book 11- Fall 2023!

Bear Grass Springs Series

Immerse yourself in 1880's Montana as the MacKinnon siblings and their extended family find love!

Montana Untamed (BGS, Book 1) Cailean and Annabelle

Montana Grit (BGS, Book 2) Alistair and Leticia

Montana Maverick (BGS, Book 3) Ewan and Jessamine

Montana Renegade(BGS, Book 4) Warren and Helen

Jubilant Montana Christmas (BGS, Book 5) Leena and Karl

Montana Wrangler (BGS, Book 6) Sorcha and Frederick

Unbridled Montana Passion (BGS, Book 7) Fidelia and Bears

Montana Vagabond (BGS, Book 8) Jane and Ben

Exultant Montana Christmas (BGS, Book 9) Ewan and Jessamine

Lassoing a Montana Heart, (BGS, Book 10)- Slims and Davina

Healing Montana Love (BGS Book 11)- Dalton and

Charlotte

Runaway Montana Groom (BGS, Book 12) Peter and Philomena

Substitute Montana Bride (BGS Book 13) Tobias and Alvira

Enraptured Montana Bachelor (BGS Book 14) Cole and Wilhelmina

Fervent Montana Devotion (BGS, Book 15) Shorty and Rose

Reluctant Montana Husband (BGS, Book 16) Nathanial and Beatrice

The Banished Saga

Follow the McLeod, Sullivan and Russell families as they find love, their loyalties are tested, and they overcome the challenges of their time. A sweeping saga set between Boston and Montana in early 1900's America.

The Banished Saga: (In Order)

Love's First Flames (Prequel)

Banished Love (Banished Saga, Book One)

Reclaimed Love (Banished Saga, Book Two)

Undaunted Love(Banished Saga, Book Three) (Part One)

Undaunted Love (Banished Saga, Book Three) (Part Two)

THE PIONEER BRIDES OF RATTLESNAKE RIDGE SERIES

Haven't read the entire series? Catch up with every book in the Pioneer Brides of Rattlesnake Ridge Series!

ACKNOWLEDGMENTS

Thank you to the my fellow authors of PBRR—it was so much fun writing this series with you!

Thank you, Jefe and Barry, for helping me with this title. I wouldn't have come up with such a wonderful title without brainstorming with you!

Thank you to my wonderful beta readers who always help me see plot holes and help me think through conundrums.

Thank you, DB, for your wonderful editing!

Thank you, Erin, for the beautiful cover!

And, finally, I couldn't do what I love without readers who love what I write. Thank you, dear reader, for always being so enthusiastic about everything I write and for taking a chance on a new series!

ALL ABOUT RAMONA

Ramona is a historical romance author who loves to immerse herself in research as much as she loves writing. A native of Montana, every day she marvels that she gets to live in such a beautiful place. When she's not writing, her favorite pastimes are fly fishing the cool clear streams of a Montana river, hiking in the mountains, and spending time with family and friends.

Ramona's heroines are strong, resilient women, the type of women you'd love to have as your best friend. Her heroes are loyal and honorable, men you'd love to meet or bring home to introduce to your family for Sunday dinner. She hopes her stories bring the past alive and allow you to forget the outside world for a while.